Pure Fear,

Sundress Publications • Knoxville, TN

Copyright © 2024 by Laura Dzubay
ISBN: 978-1-951979-67-6
LCCN: 2024943666
Published by Sundress Publications
www.sundresspublications.com

Editor: Samantha Edmonds
Managing Editor: Krista Cox
Editorial Assistant: Sarah Harshbarger
Editorial Interns: Kanika Lawton, Hedaya Hasan, Hiba Syed

Colophon: This book is set in Lora SemiBold
Cover Art: "Pure Fear" by Susanna Herrmann
Cover Design: Susanna Herrmann, Kristen Camille Ton
Book Design: Samantha Edmonds

Pure Fear, American Legend

Laura Dzubay

Acknowledgments

My deepest gratitude to the readers and editors at the journals where some of these stories first appeared:

Blue Earth Review, "Paradise"

Cimarron Review, "Cash 4 Gold"

Mid-American Review, "Will You Please Bring It Back to Me?"

Southern Humanities Review, "Natural Fit"

TIMBER, "Ophelia's Birthday" (as "Ophelia's Victory")

Table of Contents

Will You Please Bring It Back to Me?	9
Keep You	41
Cash 4 Gold	59
Natural Fit	77
Revenge on Meter Street	81
Ophelia's Birthday	113
The Summer Haunt	135
Indicative of Something Much Worse	161
Paradise	195
Pure Fear, American Legend	211

*Dedicated to Ellie Sage
and Julia Herrmann*

Will You Please Bring It Back to Me?

The little hamlet village in upstate New York decided, without needing to discuss it much, that they would not tell any of the other villages about the cell phone they'd found. It wasn't like it was going to give anybody an edge. Electricity was on its way whether the world liked it or not. What were they going to do, ship the thing off to the city and let it get taken apart? Fight over who got to keep it? If they lost the phone, they wouldn't be able to read the news. They wouldn't be able to watch *Game of Thrones*. The decision was simple.

People were so curious that at the first town hall about it, they sat in the humid church room for four hours while the girl who'd found it, the daughter of a man who tanned leather for a living and a woman who cooked and cleaned, caught them all up on what she'd learned from the hours she'd already spent on Wikipedia. She stumbled over some of the highlights while she tried to figure out what would be important to her friends, family, and neighbors. The next few decades were going to bring about another

Industrial Revolution, and people were going to get a lot better at communicating with each other, and inventions like this, a phone, were going to be part of it. There'd be automobiles on all the streets, and steel rail systems were going to sprawl across the country, and electricity was going to light up all the buildings. The girl bit her tongue on the moon landing, decided she'd let them see for themselves. She didn't think they'd believe her.

None of it, seemingly, could be prevented, and it disturbed some of the adults to have everything laid out in concrete terms: the fact that the world of one's elderly life was going to be changed from one's childhood felt different when it was no longer abstract. But the phone still mostly felt like a good thing. A box that took everything they couldn't yet know or understand, and especially couldn't control, and channeled it into clear and calm figures, dates and delineations. They hadn't realized before there was so much they didn't know; they'd just been living their lives up until now. A few of them meandered out of the church that day and kept on living their lives anyway.

The rest of them, the ones who were interested, decided to share it. They passed it around, so every interested household could have their chance to explore the future. Once a week, on Fridays, they held movie nights together, gathering in the church and propping the phone up against some Bibles where everyone could sit close and squint at it. They wound up watching *Legally Blonde* this way, and *The Empire Strikes Back*, and *Toy Story*. Propping the tiny screen up on the pulpit wasn't meant as irony; in time, some of them truly came to believe the phone was a gift from God.

At the end of that first meeting, it occurred to someone to look up their own name on the search engine the tanner's daughter had shown them, Google. Once one person did, they all did. The tanner's daughter stood there patiently and typed in the names of each person in the village, first, middle, and last. None of the names yielded any people on Google, or at least not the right people. Not themselves. At this everyone was a little confused—anything that is all-knowing, they thought, should surely know me—but they tried to look past it.

***

The girl, who was ten, was born with the name Elizabeth and went by Beth, but after she found the phone, she tried semi-successfully to get everyone in the village to call her Lindsay, like Lindsay Lohan. She loved the sound of it, a name from the future.

The battery was at eighty-three percent, and it was always at eighty-three percent. She'd found it on the side of a muddy lane, churned into a squelching rivulet after the previous night's rain. She was running to a friend's house when her foot landed against the hard, smooth corner of something rectangular. Curious, she stopped, knelt, and smeared the mud away. The light blinked on as soon as she touched it.

That first day, it wouldn't stop making sounds. Beth was terrified, then intrigued. Instead of her friend's house, she ran to the shallows of the woods and hid there all day, sitting hunched over on a noble cloak of moss draped over a nurse log. She perched there until her calves fell asleep, tapping and pressing and inspecting. On one of its loud eruptions, she figured out how to make the ringing stop, and then a boy's voice said, "Hello?"

Beth's eyes widened. It was hard to believe the voice had come from this little thing, and for a moment she thought maybe someone was out here, hiding behind a tree, playing with her from just out of sight.

"Hello?" the boy's voice said again.

"Hello?" said Beth.

"Who's that?"

"It's Beth," said Beth. "Who's that?"

"Jake." The boy sounded indignant. "What are you doing with my phone?"

"Your what?"

"My phone, stupid!"

"Don't call me stupid!" Now Beth felt angry, too. She figured the phone must be what she was holding.

"You have to give it back to me," said the boy. "It's brand new. It's my first one. I asked and asked forever—" He sounded like he was on the verge of crying.

"I didn't steal it," said Beth. She didn't like his tone. "I just *found* it."

"I don't care!" Now he was definitely crying. "I only got it a couple *days* ago. My mom said I had to be responsible—" He sniffled loudly. "Will you please bring it back to me?"

You're the one who lost it, thought Beth. "Where are you?" she asked.

"Um—" He sniffled again. "One second." Then his voice grew more muffled, and she couldn't hear any of what was being said. "Okay," the boy said after a minute, more quietly, as if he was talking to someone else. Beth looked around again, but she saw no one hiding, nothing but the age-streaked chestnut trees standing guard and watching her coolly. She couldn't attach any direction to the voice, anyway; it was coming from right there, no farther away than her hands.

"Um, can you bring it to number five-one-three Woodlawn?" the boy asked. "It's not broken or anything, is it?"

Beth frowned at the phone and turned it over in her hands. "It's a bit muddy," she said. "What's it supposed to do?"

"Um," the boy repeated, "phone calls?" When she didn't say anything, he added, "Like this one right now?"

Beth shook her head. "Then it's not broken," she said, irritated. "And I don't know where Woodlawn is."

"It's near the arcade. If you turn left at the McDonald's on the west side." His tone suggested he'd recited this information many times before.

Beth leaned back and curled her toes inside her leather shoes. She already didn't like this boy's way of talking, and she didn't want to know how he'd react if she revealed she had no sense of what an arcade was. Instead, she asked, "Where do the McDonalds live?"

Jake's voice ratcheted up into a whine. "Stop making fun of me!"

"I'm *not*!"

This was going nowhere. Beth hung up. She adjusted her position on the log and tried to ignore a stirring in her gut: a wandering feeling that what she was holding in her hand was something significant. She picked up a stick with her other hand and started scratching its tip into the dirt. The knowledge pulsed under her heart, growing slowly stronger: that no one she knew, not her parents or her neighbors or the schoolteacher or anyone else she looked up to, had seen an object like this before, and that she was taking part in one of those few moments that might live beyond her life—even if only a little beyond. She imagined this was how people felt when a man proposed, or a leader was sworn in. But she tried to keep this swirling feeling contained within her, for fear it would get away too soon.

It would be a few more frustrated conversations, a few more hours of exploring and pressing and swiping, before Beth felt fully settled within the only conclusion she could really reach: that something unexplainable had happened and she was now in possession of a machine from the future.

***

For his part, it took some convincing before Jake came to accept that Beth lived in a different time. He told her repeatedly and with much emphasis that he was in a lot of trouble with his mom for losing his phone, *and* that everyone in his class at school had a phone or at least an "iPad" so he was getting left out of a bunch of things, and when this didn't prompt her to take pity on him and return the phone, he gave up trying. Her level of confusion was also probably convincing, although frustrating, while she tried to get him to teach her what the internet was and how to use it, and then what all his app-games were and how to play them.

Over the next few days, she spent so much time acquainting herself with the phone that her mother decided she was out playing too much. She wouldn't be a little girl much longer; she needed to learn to contribute. During the mornings, Beth started helping around the house and making lunch with her mother, and in the afternoons, if they'd gotten enough done, her mother would relinquish her to go and help her father in the tannery.

The tannery was small, an addition in the front of their house where people could bring in hides for Beth's father to tan and transform into hard, shiny leather for boots, belts, satchels, and anything else people asked for. It could be an eerie place at night, with the salt-dried hides of squirrels and raccoons and deer from the woods hanging and drying in their sprawled-flat forms, tails sticking straight down. But during the day, familiar faces passed in and out, and Beth's father with his strong arms and veiny hands taught her how to soak the hides and scrape their flesh clean with the careful blade of a drawknife. Beth felt fully absorbed in her life in these hours—in the smells of tannic acid and oak and hemlock bark, in the easy rhythm of working in her father's shadow and learning how to care about a job well done.

But in her free moments—when she was in bed with exhaustion tearing at her eyelids, or when she snuck out behind the outhouse—she was scouring Wikipedia, playing Candy Crush on mute, or sneaking in conversations with Jake. The phone's camera didn't work, so she couldn't send photos or FaceTime, but they came to know each other's voices well: Jake's was high and scratchy most of the time, except for when he consciously made it sound low and reasonable.

She liked the secrecy of it, but it also made her feel selfish. She didn't like knowing things her parents and her neighbors didn't know, didn't like the kernel of self-superiority she could sense it creating in her. So when she felt ready, she took it to the town hall, and made it a town discussion.

***

It took some time for everyone to find what they liked to spend their turns on. Dr. Harmon, after a long day of healing using nostrum and opiates and home remedies, would read articles about penicillin and vaccinations and struggle in vain to understand everything they meant, and what he could possibly do, and what all this golden future-knowledge could mean for him. Some days he would simply give up and take comfort instead of the knowledge: pull his covers to his chin in bed and watch *House, M.D.* on the little rectangle of light.

The Pritchards, a farmer and his wife who lived down the lane from Beth, were old-fashioned. All they wanted was music. On their turns they played The Beatles in the early hours of the morning, Ella Fitzgerald and Nina Simone in the evenings while Mrs. Pritchard cooked dinner. Mrs. Pritchard had a beautiful singing voice, but she never showed it off to anyone but her husband, and she sang along in low breaths while she concentrated on the simmering broth in the woodstove with her narrow shoulders bent inward, and often she wouldn't notice he was listening admiringly from the doorway until he started singing along. They were otherwise a very restrained couple, known by their neighbors to smile only sparingly. But the world is full of withheld mysteries like this, pockets of truth only known and shared by one or two people, and only for a short while.

Without noticing it, the village drew in a little, became more isolated but also more unique. They did think they were special; they were proud of their democratic phone-sharing process. Maybe this wasn't what all towns would do, gifted a window into the future, but it was what this one did. Children traded crushes they'd cultivated from Google Images: Daniel Radcliffe, Kristen Stewart. Parents would say things like, "You're being such a teenager," ironic smiles tugging at the corners of their mouths.

Occasionally someone would travel to other villages and towns, or even to big cities like New York, on business or visiting relatives. They carried with them the knowledge that they'd left the future at home, secured in a rectangle. It was theirs to keep, theirs to discover. It was true they didn't have the future clothes they came to yearn for—blue jeans or Sephora makeup or tank tops or iridescent jackets—nor did they have the future inventions, the computers or TVs or refrigerators or microwaves. All they had were ideas and pictures. But an idea was all the future really was, and for right now, it was plenty.

Meanwhile, people in other towns and cities occasionally cast them odd, disapproving looks. These villagers made no sense. Some, like Beth-who-was-also-Lindsay, had refashioned themselves with names from the future. Occasionally they let slip things like LOL and *groovy* and *that's the tea!*

And back home, the adults grew addicted to the news. They were amused by the idea that over a century from now, other adults were cracking open their computers with their coffee, learning something that, little did they know, actually wasn't new at all, that—despite being long dead by then—they and their children and neighbors had secretly known for years and years.

***

Beth made Jake give her his mom's cell phone number and promise not to talk to anyone in the village but her. This was less because she'd be jealous if he made friends with anyone else and more because she wanted to keep the whole situation as much as she could within the realm of her control. It would be so easy for it all to slip away. It wasn't that she didn't trust him. It was just that he was already out of her reach.

Once, they tried going out together at the exact same time of night, to test whether they were at least looking at the same sky. Beth's mother scolded her for staying up late, but she didn't push it. Beth lay out in the field behind their house, and even though the air was chillier at night and her nightgown might get dirty, she relaxed as much as she could into the prickly grass and picked out the stars. They were all startlingly clear, scattered far across the sky like spilled flour.

"I don't see too many," said Jake.

"Well, there's our first difference," said Beth.

"How about the moon?"

"Mine's full. How's yours?"

"Ahh." Jake sounded crestfallen. "Not *quite* full."

"Well—" Beth hesitated, frowning up at the sky. Come to think of it, she wasn't sure hers was quite full, either. Maybe there was a chip off the edge of it. "I think I was wrong," she said. "Mine isn't full, either."

"So you think it's the same one?"

"I think it's the same one." She paused, then laughed. "Of course it is, we're both looking at the moon, aren't we?"

Jake was quiet for a moment. "Did Neal say he was sorry? For pulling your hair?"

"Yes." She smiled. Neal lived down the street from her and was one of those kids who did nothing all day except look for new ways to be annoying. "His parents were so mad."

"That's good." He hesitated again. "I have a question."

"Yeah?"

"Would—do you want to be my girlfriend? Maybe, for a little while?"

She pretended to think about it, but a thrill went through her. A girlfriend was like Julia Stiles in 10 *Things I Hate About You*. She grinned at the phrase *for a little while*. "Sure. What do I have to do?"

"Nothing. We'll just talk like we talk already, only—well, I can tell Aaron and Miranda I have a girlfriend." She could hear him smiling. Aaron and Miranda were his school friends; Beth was up to date on their whole saga.

"Okay." She pulled up a tuft of grass with her fist and sprinkled it down across her chest. "I'll tell Neal I have a boyfriend," she said, and smiled, because it did make her happy even though it didn't mean anything.

***

Jake broke his promise to her one time, out of curiosity. The baker was returning the phone to Beth with an amused smile on his face, and he said, "Your little friend from the future called."

"*What?* Ugh! I'm going to kill him!" Beth said. She had just picked up this phrase from the previous Friday's movie.

When she called Jake and confronted him, he laughed and said, "C'mon, Beth. A village full of people trading a phone around? I kind of just thought you lived down the street."

"I told you to call me Lindsay," she said tearfully, and hung up. He texted her the whole rest of the day, frowny faces and heart emojis, until she finally called him back.

***

Of course it was bound to sour; once the future feels like the present, and you realize you can't get the old present back, it always sours. They wanted TVs. They wanted toasters. They wanted back the ability to not want TVs and toasters. They wanted cures to the diseases that in that time could set upon someone so randomly. It felt unspeakably dumb to know about the wars and tragedies they would have to live through, like the ones they'd already lived through, like the ones their parents and grandparents had lived through and told them stories about—most of them wouldn't help anyone; they would just leave people dead or bloody and fill up ink in textbooks a hundred years down the line. Couldn't they just skip them?

Friday movie nights began to ebb in attendance, and some neighbors started disavowing the phone, or forbidding their children to use it. Some clung to it harder. Dr. Harmon started returning it with stiff looks on his face, looking more and more haunted with the passing months.

Meanwhile, Jake got into the habit of complaining at length about politics and the general problems of his own world. To Beth it felt like listening to the recurring plot threads of a TV show—while she was sure, to Jake, talking to her probably felt like dipping his toes into a historical drama. He told her when they legalized gay marriage, and how all the elections went, and when the surprise albums dropped.

Another time, later—Beth's energy drained anew at the end of each day as she grew older, her head swimming with woodsmoke and legs and arms rippling with exhaustion and hunger, muscles hewn close to her bones—"Did you know Charlie Heaton and Natalia Dyer are dating in real life?"

"Wow," said Beth, rubbing her calloused palm into one eye to massage the headache away. Food was scarce this spring, and everyone was scrambling to keep up; many nights she felt like she was scrambling her way even through her dreams, waking up again bone-tired, all of it pointless.

"Sometimes I feel like you think everything in my world is trivial," said Jake, sounding hurt. "Just because it can't touch you."

"You say that like we don't live in the same world," said Beth, even though she knew she was being dense. They didn't live in the same world.

When he broke up with her that winter, she wasn't particularly surprised or particularly disappointed. She called him a day off schedule because the preacher had been hogging the phone, and one of the first things out of his mouth was, "It's not you, it's just, it's hard for me to do the long-distance thing."

She knew she could get over the sting of being broken up with, but she did feel she had to justify herself. "Do you know how much work I have to do to feel like I can keep up with you? With the way you talk, with the references you make? On top of, like, my real-life chores, and work, and my real-life—*life*. How much do you know about my world?"

"That's different," said Jake. "Everyone from my time knows about your time."

"Do they?"

"I mean, yeah, we can look it up."

"That's not the same!"

"How is it not the same? Aren't you looking up stuff about my time?"

Beth stewed, trying to latch upon the source of her anger. "It's just—it's just—you think you know so much. You think you're so beyond us. And you're *not*—you're just somewhere else."

He laughed at that—actually laughed. "Yeah, somewhere a hundred and fifty years ahead of you."

She was startled by this meanness, too startled to speak at first. He'd never been mean before.

"I'm sorry. That came out—I didn't mean that in, like, a bad way," he amended. Then he added, quickly, "I'm not a jerk."

"At least we *know* about our future," said Beth. "We have answers about what's going to happen. You don't have anything."

Jake was quiet for a moment again, but when he spoke, he didn't sound defeated. He sounded like he felt guilty for having an answer. "We know some of it," he said.

"What are you talking about?"

"I mean, the climate stuff, for one," he said. "You know?"

Beth knew, in a general sense. She still had a lot to learn—about everything, really. But she remembered the day she'd learned how the glaciers were going to melt, and how the rainforests would shrink, and the oceans and lakes would fill up with smoke and poison. The stars would be blotted out, snow would stop falling, and someday, long after humanity's food and hope ran out, the sun would explode. She supposed that was one thing her time had that Jake's didn't—all those species that for now were still focused on thriving and evolving, and by his time would already be forever extinct, and never able to be gotten back. The passenger pigeon. The heath hen.

"Yeah, but—" She felt unsure of herself now. "That's a long time away, right?"

"Not really," said Jake. "Some of it's already happening. We're already doing it. Our kids, our grandkids." He said *our*, even though he really meant his—for Beth, they would be great-grandkids, great upon great upon great.

He spoke so indifferently, she felt like there must be something she wasn't getting. "You say it like you're doing it on *purpose*."

"We are," said Jake. Then he backtracked again: "I mean—not—just, we've *known* for a while now. Like, a really long time. So at this point, yeah, it must be on purpose."

There was a simmer in Beth's head, building to a boil. "Don't you *care*?"

"Of course I care," said Jake, and she was surprised to hear anger in his voice. "A lot of us care. We just can't do much. People don't listen. And besides, we've been screwed already, by the people who came before us."

"Oh, the people who came before you," said Beth flatly. She stood up again and looked through the trees, thinning into leafless bars with the wintertime. She looked at the sun until it burned her eyelids and then looked away.

"That's not what I meant," said Jake. Now he sounded ashamed. "You just don't know what it's like."

Jake who'd never rationed out a winter, Jake who'd never tanned a hung deerskin or mended anything in his life. She tried to imagine the day-to-days of his world, a world defined by refrigerator magnets and social media and skyscrapers and Sour Patch Kids and Flamin' Hot Cheetos, but also by fear and the knowledge that right at the moment you were eating all those foreign flavors Beth would never taste, millennia-old birds and frogs and foxes and trees were dying. Literally dying, never to breathe again. She wondered if Jake was trying to imagine what it was like where she was, too. She knew he probably was, knew he probably had many times.

"I know it's not *your* fault," said Jake. "It's been a lot of people along the line, but it wasn't you."

Beth sighed. She knew what he wanted to hear, and it was probably decently true, so she said it. "It wasn't you, either."

Across the centuries they were both holding the phone with both hands, their mouths pressed into hard lines. Eventually Jake laughed, sadly, nervously. "You know, I was just trying to break up with you," he said.

***

Jake and Beth tried to stay friends for a while. They went through phases when they didn't talk, but always drifted back together. Out of nowhere, pangs of sentimentality would send them calling each other in the middle of the afternoon, awkward and shy at first but always ultimately encouraging of each other, reassured by the comfort that only the voice of a close childhood friend can really bring. They'd catch each other up on life events and school drama, the latest episodes of *Killing Eve*. Closeness can have its own kind of feeling for children, a feeling of discovering life in tandem, and not every phone call tapped them back into that closeness, but each one was a reminder, a recognition. To

Beth, it started to feel like a million years ago that she'd been a child.

Eventually something happened—maybe Jake's mom missed a payment on the cell phone bill, or the carrier disbanded—and he stopped calling. Beth preferred to think it was one of these things, something mundane, rather than that something had happened to Jake. Maybe he'd just gone too long without calling, and somehow managed to forget the number he'd spent his entire childhood dialing, his own number, and maybe he'd stood somewhere for hours punching in random numbers, combinations of ones and threes and eights that almost felt familiar, grasping for the right one and coming up with stranger after stranger. Beth waited awhile, and when she eventually called his mom's cell phone number it didn't work; the phone would no longer call anyone.

The percent was still at eighty-three, and the internet still worked. Beth sat in bed with her mother and cried, and they watched a cheesy movie until Beth's cheeks were dry, her head post-crying-fuzzy, and her mother's arm had fallen asleep behind her back.

She started foregoing her phone time. She spent more hours at the tannery, acquainting her skin with the tiny nicks of the blade, feeling her hands become calloused and gamey. She didn't mind smelling of leather and lime solution, because that was the way her father smelled. She learned the best ways to curry the leather and smoke it, and how to sew the final products into durable goods that would last a lifetime. She felt as if she were growing stronger, but she had always been strong—maybe she was only growing bigger, beginning to fill the kind of space and attention in the world that adults filled.

Even though the phone could still do some things, it started taking on a nostalgic feeling for Beth—a relic that no longer told her new things, only offered repetitions and reminders of things about the world she already knew.

And anyway, there were still parts of the future she could see, scattered all around her. Saplings that would one day be red oaks and maples and beeches, where squirrels scampered and warblers and woodpeckers nested, and shade spread out and rain caught itself in loud rushes and kids played hide-and-seek, and eventually loggers arrived to chop them down. Every person she met and loved was going to stay in the world forever and ever, even if they had to do it only as bones and dust. Every night she saw a moon that would one day be walked on. How might those astronauts feel, thinking about how even as they stepped onto that rock, her eyes had hit that land centuries earlier and *known*?

Gradually Beth started to get the feeling she might need to get away for a little while. Not necessarily forever, but sometime, and soon. She knew it was a little *basic bitch* of her to need to go out and see the world, and she already knew she loved her little hometown, which had become so strange these last few years, giving space to things that wouldn't be real for years to come. But she also knew for a fact there was so much else out there, and the time was approaching when she would need to see it with her own eyes.

She delayed as long as she really could, until the day that was always bound to come—the day she had no other option.

***

She knew when the doctor didn't give the phone back. She didn't know how she hadn't known earlier: He'd fallen into a deep depression in the years since the phone's appearance, and rather than developing his practice with the new knowledge at his fingertips, he'd actually started dropping the ball. He was distracted, glassy-eyed, and sometimes downright inadequate. A few months earlier, Mrs. Richardson had quietly ridden to Buffalo to deliver her baby there rather than try to rely on Dr. Harmon at home.

Mrs. Harmon wouldn't say anything except that her husband had gone to New York City, and that he'd said people would "know what to do with it there". That was enough to set Beth going. If she'd learned one thing from the phone, it was that people would not know what to do with it.

She told the schoolteacher's teenage son she'd pay him all the pocket money she had saved to drive her to the city and back. In the carriage, she watched as the countryside ticked by, the furrows of grain rising and falling and the long driveways spooling out between red barns and grain silos, pockmarked by spokes in the road and bales of hay. Clouds murmuring their way across the blue sky. She wondered how soon the railway might be through here. For her purposes, today, it didn't matter.

The city when she arrived was smokier than the rest of the state or anywhere she was used to. There were no skyscrapers yet, nothing taller than ten or so stories, but what was there was still thick with industry: carts rattling down the lanes, horses' hooves clipping over silver cobblestone, people traveling in close flocks and laughing and calling out to one another. Some people had put out hats and cups for passersby to deposit their spare change, while vendors stood nearby selling fruits and inventions and pastries, and pushing bright popcorn carts with striped coverings. Children screamed and chased after one another and ate roasted pecans and peanuts out of oily paper bags, and all around them these buildings stretched up with their crisp red brick sides, shining windows, and stern, stone-columned facades. People glaring at each other, people winking at each other, people bustling past and into and out of shop doors that jangled with declaration. Every inch of it was startling. But it was startling in a way that set something inside Beth alight, with wonder or trepidation, she didn't know and probably would never decide. Someone somewhere was playing a violin.

    She asked a few people where to find the nearest hospital, and they pointed her toward Bellevue. She set off that way down the lively streets, through the burgeoning neighborhoods and scarcely formed districts, her footsteps drumming in her ears along with her heartbeat. She wasn't sure if this was what Dr. Harmon would do, but it was what *she* would do. She'd even thought, many times, of how she would do it: seek out some doctor or even politician, someone high up who could connect her with whoever was at the very top, whoever had that ultimate power she really needed: the power to make it all stop. She'd recited in her head the pitch she might give them, using her clearest, most reasonable voice: *These are the facts and there's no need for you to argue about them or not believe me. Just listen. We still have time. If we play our cards right. The Arctic doesn't have to melt; these forests don't need to be gutted; even, look, this war doesn't need to be fought, and this person should under no circumstances be elected, and these people here don't have to starve; these people here don't have to die, and this world doesn't have to die; believe it or not, we don't really have to kill anything.*

And they'd call her naïve, while she held the plain proof of all this right in her hand.

Because she'd thought about how it would play out, too. She thought about it again now, as she turned the corner and the brick face of Bellevue rose into her sight, stark metal fire escapes staggering past its eyelid windows. The people she wanted to warn about the harm they might do, they already knew. The people who'd done harm in the past and died before she'd ever been born, they had known; the people who were doing it right now, knew they were doing it; and a century and a half from now, in Jake's time, they would keep knowing and most of them would keep on doing it, or keep on not stopping it from happening. They should not need a secret invention to tell them something as simple as what was wrong and what was right. If the magic of the future was to be so misused, the least Beth could do was not give it a head start. What mattered—what was good about it—she and her loved ones already carried.

She collided with Dr. Harmon only a block from the hospital. For a moment both of them were too surprised to do anything but stagger back from each other, her in her plain brown traveling dress, him in his wrinkled semblance of a coat.

The doctor was not in good shape. His hair was uneven and his eyes vacant, as though he hadn't had a full night's sleep in days. He ducked his gaze as soon as he recognized Beth, whose frail seven-year-old arm he'd once carefully arranged inside a fashioned sling, in the dry cool of his home office years ago, which had smelled distinctly of talcum even with the windows open.

"Beth," he started. "Or, ah, Lindsay." He laughed, then instantly sobered. "I can't—I hope you know, it's not—"

"I know." She took a halting step forward.

"I can't—"

She waited for him to say something: *I can't live like this*, or maybe *I can't decide*. But what he evidently could not do was explain. He started backing away from her and toward the hospital, his eyes wide and his left hand plunged protectively inside his coat pocket. Just as he angled to turn away from her, she lunged.

"What are you *doing*—" He tried shaking her off, but only really gave it the effort of one elbow. Her hand dove to his pocket and right away she felt the hard edge of the phone, recognized the feel of it the way she had years ago in the mud.

He grabbed her arm as she started pulling away. "*Stop it!*"

"You don't know what they'll do," she tried to explain. His hands were on hers, and it was hard to keep her grip. "If the wrong person—"

"Be an adult about this—"

"—but you didn't even *ask* me what I—"

"Beth, you don't—just—get to—"

And then it fell. They heard a brief clatter and then nothing. So many crucial things go this way, submerged in accidents in the blink of a moment. Together they looked down, and there it was: the storm gutter, an open hole beneath their feet.

***

They moved numbly back through the city, taking in images and having nothing to connect them with: a black bird jutting across the sky before the smokestacks, a smartly dressed woman arguing with a man in a suit in front of the golden-limned window of a department store. Beth thought about Jake—if he was way out there somewhere, still, wishing he had a way to reach her. She hoped he was living his life, and happy. Maybe by some miracle his phone would find its way back to him, even though she knew it was not really his phone any longer.

It was only on the long way home, watching a deer settle for a moment in the reeds beside a creek where the sun glinted, just before the entire creek jerked out of sight, that the numbness began to clear its way from Beth's heart. Gradually, with Dr. Harmon sitting listlessly across from her and the frame of the carriage rattling around them, she arrived at the feeling that she really had more faith in the world than she'd ever had—and less reason for her faith than anyone else alive. A future would come. And no matter what else, it would at least still have good people in it, good enough that she'd mourn not getting to talk to them and know them.

But there was plenty of work still to do here. Having knowledge, you can do anything, and she considered herself blessed that all she had really done was use it to recognize her loved ones. Maybe, she thought, that was it—to look for ourselves in things that don't see us or care for us, live like it's all precious anyway, soak in the sun as if we trust it. Record everything, in our hearts and in our consciousnesses, because the things that we're recording, nobody else will ever be this close to again.

Years later, a couple would be fishing while their son played music from a portable speaker in the grass when their daughter, swiping a net around in the water for sea creatures, would come up with a phone clogged with mud. It would be next year's model of the iPhone, not yet released. The daughter would clean it off with a leaf and set it down there in case whoever had lost it came back looking. The family would have no idea where it had come from—the same way they didn't know where the fish they caught on their hooks had come from, or the sun that warmed their backs, or the instruments that played from the latest in portable speaker technology. All of it arrived to them from the same pool, somewhere upstream where all these things lived their own lives for a while— that place they did not question, that had given them everything they would ever have.

Keep You

The tree-covered mountains, banked with snow from the night before, stood like a drawing someone had etched in ink and charcoal, like an Ansel Adams photo, like a document from a story recorded hundreds of years before the city Ann worked in existed. There were no good comparisons, really, but she turned them over in her head anyway, trying to occupy herself. The sight of it was creeping into the car, haunting her where she sat, cliffing like smoke through the car window and into her dark eyes.

The evening was growing blue and grainy when the Jeep skidded off the road. Ann seized the steering wheel and pumped the brakes, not slamming, but the car didn't regain enough traction; it slid out from the tire tracks engraved in the ice and onto a wide lookout shoulder, where it finally juddered to a stop just inches away from the edge where the road met the tree line.

Ann gripped the wheel, leaning forward with wide, strained eyes. But she was fine, she thought. Fine, fine.

The car was perpendicular to the road now. She might be able to get back on, but she wasn't sure now whether she wanted to.

She'd been driving all day, and only made it about seventy miles. Traffic had been backed up at the last town, with several cars ahead of her turning back after waiting hours at a standstill. One woman had driven past Ann with her window down, making a cutting-her-throat motion to the stopped cars as she passed them. "It's closed," she shouted through the winter air, "the pass is closed."

So Ann had turned back twenty miles, found a Safeway and eaten a sandwich in the parking lot with her heat on, trying to come up with a plan. Fuck it, she'd thought eventually—it seemed like a clear day, she could at least try again—and when she'd approached the pass a second time, the standstill had cleared, and the roads were wide open. Not a car in sight. Back then, with the sun still gleaming off the fresh fallen snow, driving had felt fine. She didn't see any state troopers, didn't know what the woman had been talking about.

She drove over the mountain most weekends, but scarcely this late at night. Colin didn't like her commuting, and he made it no secret; he always said she was in danger of getting herself stranded somewhere, and then he'd have to stop whatever he was doing and come and rescue her. Which he'd be fine doing, obviously, if it weren't such an avoidable problem—if she weren't so stupid. Not that *she* was stupid, he'd clarified the last time they'd fought about it—just a few days ago, when over breakfast they'd seen the forecast for this weekend's winter storm—of course not, why did she always take things in the worst possible way—he just meant it was a stupid thing to *do*, driving these roads in the winter, let alone several times a week.

The real anger had come when she'd gotten an apartment so she had a place to stay during the week. She'd taken pains to make sure they had a nice day before bringing it up—going for a hike together in the brittle cold, packing caprese sandwiches to eat in the car and a thermos of hot chocolate. And he'd been receptive, at first. Getting an apartment made sense, he conceded, at least more sense than her driving.

But then he'd gone to the gym late at night, to clear his head, and the next day he'd barely spoken to her. Her throat had been tight all day, constricted from the lack of conversations. A dread she couldn't name or pinpoint. He hadn't even been around that day, or said anything—it wasn't even his fault, really—and around three o'clock while having her coffee, she'd just started crying.

That had been two weekends ago. Last weekend had been full of fighting, and this week they were only exchanging perfunctory texts: *I'll probably get in around 9; OK see u soon.* But they'd both been angry long enough that it was starting to feel stale; she was tired. She was bringing a bottle of cabernet, and she was going to smile an irrefusable smile and wrap her arms around him the moment she saw him, not give either of them time for any other kind of contact. *I want the good Colin tonight*, she'd told herself while marching out of work, *and I am getting him.*

Driving always gave her a hopeful feeling, or at least a feeling of being in control. She'd been making this drive since long before they'd fallen in love, and she had other feelings stacked up in these mountains from her childhood, from high school, from college. When she drove here alone, she could think about whatever she wanted, her other feelings attached to these woods sifting down over her like layers of snowfall and covering all her thoughts of Colin: a feeling like she was a kid again, or someone wandering through a fairy tale with no surrounding context, like things were simple. If the roads were rough, she could use snow tires, she could slow down. If she got too afraid, she could stop.

Except now she *was* stopped.

She forced herself to recline; her back hurt from hunching over the wheel. She tried testing the acceleration and was met with an ugly spinning sensation from under the belly of the car. The back of the Jeep fishtailed, and she quickly braked again and put it in park. The front hadn't moved.

She breathed into her hands to warm them, tugged her scarf haphazardly from the passenger seat and around her neck, slipped on her gloves, and got out.

It was as she'd feared. Her tires were mired in snow; it was thicker on the shoulder, and her Jeep didn't want to move.

She muttered a curse and looked around the side of the mountain. There were some other smudged tracks around the lookout point—maybe other cars had gotten stuck here earlier—but there was no one around to help her now. Outside of the car, the near-single-digits cold swept around her, and the trees fanned out oppressively, reinforced by bluing shadows. The piney branches sagged under drooping piles of snow, like sheet-draped ghost costumes interspersed among the trunks. Far below in the dark, a twisting river was visible.

She bent down unceremoniously and started scooping handfuls of snow from around the tires. For several minutes, the only sounds were the soft panting of Ann's breath, the wet shuffling of chunks of snow, and the brush of cool air through the trees, here and there unsettling the white-weighted branches.

Then a pair of headlights appeared, and a car came slowly around the bend.

Ann stopped to squint through the new light. She hesitated—it was better, she thought, in a remote area like this, to just look like you know what you're doing, you never know who might come along—but the car pulled over anyway, and a man got out.

"Looks like you hit a snag!" he called, trudging towards her in his snow boots. He had a gruff, warm voice.

It was getting too dark to make out the specificities of his face, but she could see that he had a beard and wore snow pants and a reddish flannel under a thick winter coat. He was dressed very well for the weather, like he'd been out hiking or snowshoeing earlier, or like he'd been expecting to get stuck.

"Yeah, kind of." Ann tried to echo his tone and his smile. "I've got snow tires, but—"

"Oh, yeah," he said, reaching her car and examining the stuck tires. He kicked one of them lightly with the toe of a boot. "Yeah, these won't cut it."

Ann was a little annoyed, but she could put up with a little annoyance if it got her back on the road faster. "I've driven up here a lot before," she said, in an offhand way that was meant not to feel too personal. "This is the first time this has happened."

The man acted like he hadn't heard her. He stood there and stared at her tires for a minute longer, his thick-gloved hands on his hips, and then inhaled sharply like he'd made a decision. "All right, wait here a sec," he said, turning back toward his own car, "I'm gonna get you hooked up."

"Hooked—hooked up?"

She was about to tell him she didn't want to be towed or anything—that felt like way more of an ordeal than this demanded—but when he returned, he was carrying a fistful of snow chains. His headlights were still on, and the thin metal gleamed as he carried them back towards her.

"Oh, you don't have to do that. I don't want to take them from you—"

"Nonsense!"

He handed her two of the balled-up chains. There might have been a moment there to push them back, but she didn't take it; she let her grip go slack, closed her fingers just in time to accept.

"Are you sure?"

"Don't ask me again, or I'll change my mind! Here, I'll take this side."

Ann crossed to the far side of her car and knelt to start applying the chains, one knee dampening into the snow. She'd been out for a while now, and her neck and ears were starting to feel itchy and red, her nose runny, her toes numb inside too-thin tennis shoes.

It was a kind thing for a stranger to do. She might've been touched by it if she wasn't so focused on feeling cold and uncomfortable. She probably wouldn't tell Colin about it later; he'd ask all the wrong questions, like, *Why didn't you have good snow tires to begin with?* and *What the fuck were you doing alone on that mountain?* Even though if she'd decided not to try coming, if she'd turned back and spent the weekend in her apartment, he would've been furious.

She was doing it again, now. Blaming him for fights they hadn't even had. She flexed her fingers; even through the thin gloves, the metal chains were making them sting.

"Yep," the man said a few minutes later, as if they'd been talking. He stood up and brushed some gritty snow and ice off his gloves. "That's the problem with those Jeeps. They look like they're strong, but they're not."

"I guess." Ann stood, too, on the other side of the car. She was finished with the chains. Now that she was standing, the foreboding beauty of the mountainside struck her again: Even as night fell, none of the black looked quite black—the white from the snow remained, insistent, enthralling everything. The settling darkness took away all but the snow.

Looking down the slope, she saw that a large gap opened between the trees just ahead of her. The trees were tall enough to make the passageways between them look cavernous, like she was standing now at the bottom of a giant trench.

Here, outside the car, she felt even more like she was in a story. Like if she just walked straight down that corridor of woods, she could find witches living in fire-warmed huts, bears to befriend and follow home to their dens, foxes to bestow gifts upon her, wolves who'd share secrets with her and guide her from path to path. If only she were the right type of creature, she could live here.

"Nope," the man said, in the same tone he'd used to say *yep*. "It's certainly not too fun. No, *fun* isn't the word I'd use."

She looked over at him. "What's not fun?"

He gave her a smile. Was it mean, she thought—or ungrateful—to think of his smile as looking a little crooked?

"It's a tough drive," she said—although she got the feeling as she said it that she was covering something up, that the man had maybe meant something else. She felt the need to keep going. "It's beautiful, though. Right?"

"What, you're not sure?"

"No, I'm sure."

The man watched her for a moment longer and then laughed. "Beautiful, I don't know. It's cold. That's one thing it is."

"Right." She shook her thoughts loose. She felt she should walk back around the car to the driver's side, and she started to, but then she stopped at the bumper. For some reason she still wanted just a little space between the two of them.

"Well, thank you so much," she said. "I know it's cold, and you've got places to be. I didn't mean to keep you."

"Sure you didn't mean to get kept, either." He shook his head again. "It's not a great place to get stuck, I'll tell you that. But the snow—the snow'll do that." He paused for a moment and exhaled loudly, his breath curling cold in front of him. Then he added, "Get you so you're either stuck too still or moving too fast!"

Too late, she realized he was making a joke, and tried to salvage the moment with a laugh. He didn't return the laugh, just made a hoarse kind of sigh, so she wasn't sure if it worked.

They both lingered a moment longer. The man seemed like he didn't want to get back in his own car anymore.

"All right," Ann said heavily, "well—"

The man, luckily, turned out to be fluent in *all right, well*. "All right, well, you get home safe, now. All right?"

"Okay! Thank you again!"

She ducked back inside her car before he could change his mind, then flipped the engine on, praying the car would get going again. She gently accelerated and found her tires easing forward, the chains rotating between the rubber and the ice. The car gathered movement and traction, and she heard the man whooping in victory, still standing just outside his own car, and she rolled her window down so she could cheer with him as she got back on the road.

And she was off! Wonderful, she thought.

By the time she rounded the next bend and the other car's headlights winked away behind her, the man still didn't appear to have kept driving. Wonderful, wonderful.

The next few miles rolled smoothly beneath and around her. It was full dark now, and crags and exposed tree trunks poked out of the snow below the road, near the river, in a hunched way that made them look like people. Ahead of Ann, lines of wood between the snow piles were so thin and scarce that the road looked like it wound through a narrow rock canyon, rather than a forest, so thick and high was the snow on both sides of the road. The snow tires with the chains on rumbled louder than usual, drowning out the bitten static of the radio. She breathed into her hands periodically and felt herself warming up a little, the red in her knuckles and ear cartilage and raw cheeks beginning to thaw out.

Gradually, her feeling of victory ebbed. She felt bad about the anxiety that had begun creeping over her back there, in the cold. The man had been very nice, giving her his snow chains—shouldn't she have offered him some money? She only had a few dollars in cash, but it was the nice thing to do, at least offering, and she hadn't even thought of it. The right thing to do was not only good but also simple and easy, and it hadn't even crossed her mind.

Also, she wasn't even at the pass yet. Even with the chains, it was going to take ages to get home. Colin would be up waiting for her.

It's like you're soft-breaking-up with me. Two out of seven days of the week—that's like a fourth of the time, I get to see you.

It came from a place of caring about her, she knew. But he was right, and something about it felt unfair, and preemptively sad. The fraction of her that existed in relation to him was shrinking and shrinking; she was somewhere else, letting something else start to consume her, and worst of all, she didn't think she even realized it except in fleeting moments. In place of Colin's love, she didn't know what new force might be free to envelop her, or whether it would be a good or a bad one.

He still loved her, even right at this moment supposedly, but she couldn't feel his love. All the attention on her right now felt like it was coming from the mountain, bearing down these dark, winding paths where no one could see her.

She came over the top of a downward slope so steep she stuck her tongue down in front of her teeth. When she'd made it almost all the way down, her headlights hit the back of a man walking down the road, his gloved thumb stuck out on his left.

She took care not to slam on her brakes, and a shudder passed through her. A hitchhiker—alone, here? Tonight? She hadn't seen any other stopped cars—no cars at all, not since town. Except that one.

No one stops to help hitchhikers these days—not really, thought Ann. People were too untrustworthy. And it was an inconvenience. She had a place where she was going, and a time she had to get there by, and she was already late. And then what if she couldn't get him to his destination? She'd just carry him for a while and then dump him back out in the cold?

All the same, she slowed down. For a moment, she had the wild thought that he might be the same nice man who had helped her earlier—although, no, he would've been behind her, right? And then as she drew closer and rolled down her window, he tilted his head her way and she saw his face, and her heart jolted. It wasn't the same man. He smiled at her.

What was different—the shape of his beard? The lengths of his eyebrows? The structure of his eyes and nose? Somewhere between these lay the answer, but he had really looked eerily similar from behind, and somehow still did, despite her knowing as she looked at him that it was not the same man. She pressed on the gas, so suddenly the car almost skidded, and a moment later he was gone, eaten up behind her.

She sat in silence for the next few minutes while she drove. Why was her heart beating like that? She needed to concentrate better, at least until she hit the gravel.

It was several minutes before she realized a cold wind had been blowing past her, chilling the right side of her face and turning her ear red, tangling her hair in her ponytail. She rolled back up the window.

She kept shuttling onward, nestled between the four-foot-tall snowbanks and their bumpy crests. She imagined being of the snow, of the pine: finding herself trapped here, somehow, not necessarily as Ann, not necessarily as human, with some company that was maybe not necessarily kind bears and foxes.

Far below the road, the river lay like a black eel. The shapes on the slope across it, which had been like paintings, or photographs, or records whispering to her from another time, were only shadows now, watching closely from the tops of the nearest hills. Directly beside the road, thin trees stood piled with snow, like bare ribcages of bleached bones. Skeletal limbs forking out—

My god, *stop* it, thought Ann, and shook out her shoulders.

Beneath her wheels, the road turned to gravel. Here it was—the pass. The highest point. Stars stuck across the sky above her, watching her through the cold branches.

I'm in control. The thought felt like a fragment in her head; she felt small, holding the steering wheel. She passed a snow-capped brown sign marking the turnoff for a campground, which during warmer months was probably well visited, but today the trail road looked undriveable.

Then, just as she was rounding the last stretch, another figure crested into her view, a hunched-over man walking ahead of her on the road. Not again, she thought. The same man—the same coat. Where was his car?

She had a feeling this would be the last time she'd see him. It would be her last chance—but to do what? Clouds were gathering overhead, stealthily, all too dark to see. The road was keeping her such a secret up here, between the woods and the sky and the river. Her last chance for what? She had the feeling she might never get an answer—that the answer would not be handed over to her, like snow chains, as easy as a physical miracle. If she wanted it at all, she'd have to seek it out, would have to trudge out after it through a crystallizing dark.

And as much as, for a second now, that truth felt like breath in her lungs, she knew she was going home tonight, and she likely wouldn't. She had someone to apologize to. She had sadness to inhale, and a driveway to pull into under the warm lights.

And suddenly her headlights weren't on the stranger anymore, and he was gone into the dark. He must be behind her, walking after her in the same direction. Out of sight, out of mind, she thought—only really, on the contrary, she now felt like he could be anywhere.

In the race between him and the morning, who'd chase the other away? When the pink sun rose and brightened all the snow again, would he still be here to squint at it, and feel cold under it, and march through it until it slipped away again? Or would someone like him melt away with the darkness, the way wolves did?

She couldn't know now. There'd been some juncture where her feeling safe and good and certain could have been possible, and she had a creeping feeling she'd passed it. And an even worse feeling that maybe she hadn't at all, and it would never leave her—that that juncture would lurk upon her shoulders for years and years, everywhere she went, always there but never presenting itself to her.

Nothing happened, she told herself as she edged down the mountain. She knew how she'd relay the night to Colin once she got in: The roads were bad, some people thought they were closed but they seemed open to me, I had a little skidding at one point, but a nice man let me use his snow chains. Nothing had happened which was worth being creeped out by, which was how she felt now. Hitchhikers were supposed to attack you if you stopped for them, if you were alone and too dumb, or too kind. It didn't make sense that you would decide to pass right by them, and they'd haunt you anyway.

  Later in the night, snow began to fall again, relentless, like disparate white waves crushing into the hull of a ship. Ann kept her eyes firmly on the road from then on out, refusing to let her attention deviate although she felt something cold and soft pulling at her from all directions.

Cash 4 Gold

When I was around thirteen, my mother's ex-boyfriend picked me up from school and drove me not to my neighborhood, but out to the main highway that carried on north toward Fernandina. We left the dregs of the city and sailed onward up the ratty road, palm trees fluttering along its frayed edges and thrumming with the promise of rain. It took me about twenty minutes to realize that I was being kidnapped.

My mom's ex-boyfriend's name was Con or Conny, short for Lincoln. He hated it when people called him Link. Back when they were dating, which lasted about four years, he used to take me for fun little excursions around town, just the two of us on an adventure: Conny and Callie taking over the world. Splashing in the shallows at the public beach, slamming go-karts together at Adventure Landing. Lincoln was either a freelancer or a lowlife drifter, depending on my mother's mood. When my mom had broken up with him about a year earlier, he'd been working at a Smoothie King.

He didn't say a word after we pulled out of the school parking lot, after the initial *Hi*

Callie, it's me, your old pal Conny, I'm picking you up today. I'd been puzzled but happy to see him, hadn't asked questions. For several minutes after pulling onto the highway we sat in silence, and I wondered, bumping up and down in the rickety passenger seat of his pickup, what was the proper thing to say after you realize you've been kidnapped. I felt that bringing it up directly might make him mad, to be accused of something so obviously tasteless. Nobody wants to be a kidnapper. But at this point, every minute another mile between us and town, to politely ask, *Is this just a different way of getting home than normal?* would be dumb and probably pointless.

Shuttling above the Riverside Arts Market on an overpass, I decided Smoothie King would be a good access point. It was conversational, innocuous. I asked him, "Are you still working at Smoothie King?"

Lincoln blinked a few times and looked over at me as though just then remembering I was there. "Ah, no," he said regretfully. "Layoffs. That shit, you know, it fluctuates so much with the seasons."

"Sure," I said, as if I could relate personally.

Lincoln wore an extra-large stained Carhartt jacket that was big even for him, and which I knew without having to lean over would smell like Lincoln himself: musty, warm, cigarettes stamped over time into something not gross but familiar. It was the same smell of his truck, in which I now found myself, doors locked.

I looked at the digital numbers indicating the time just below the dashboard: 4:17. Twenty minutes from school, in the wrong direction; thirty-five minutes from home.

Lincoln saw me looking and misunderstood. "Oh, sorry," he said. "You wanna listen to the radio? We can listen to the radio."

I looked at him. His nails had gone grimy, clutching the ends of his jacket sleeves atop the shredded-up steering wheel. His cheeks were reddish and his eyes were shiny with a distraught film. I wasn't about to say no.

My lips formed again around the word, *Sure*, but no sound came out. Lincoln turned up the volume and found a station anyway, "You're Gonna Make Me Lonesome When You Go" by Bob Dylan.

***

I didn't own a cell phone. My mother was one of those traditional parents. Not in every way—like she'd debate me about stuff we saw on the news, and when we did go out on our rare, special shopping days, she'd take me to any store I wanted, no questions asked. Aeropostale, Hot Topic, these were distinct realms to a lot of the other kids at school and therefore, I knew, to their parents as well, but it was all the same to her. What mattered was that I, a young teenage girl vulnerable every day to the pressures and hatreds of a wide and evil world, felt free to express myself.

Expressing myself through texts was a different story. My mother loved bringing up the seventies, that golden era back when the beaches had been less crowded and people still listened to The Beatles all the time, and she was a firm believer that my generation would be better off if we all spent a lot less time *hooked up to our devices*. I had to wait until I was ten to even get an email account—each year, each month, was excruciatingly long—and a phone was out of the question until high school. I was always looped into group plans at the last minute, always grinning awkwardly at the end of some in-joke. My mother saw this as character-building, that I would never need to rely on technology to communicate with other people. That was always the word: not talking, *communicating*.

My friends at school were Sam, Evana, Jessica. They didn't mind that I couldn't text them—it wasn't their problem—and they all liked my mom. From their softball field and subdivision vantages they thought she was adventurous. *Amy,* they'd plead, *tell us about that time before Callie was born when you drove to Atlanta and blacked out. Tell us about when you hitchhiked to California.* Sometimes, us all having had sleepovers together since elementary, they called her Aunt Amy, a jokey habit that somewhat annoyed but also oddly pleased me.

What they really meant by all of this was *Tell us about your men.* Because that's what my mom's stories were: Her ex-boyfriends figured in each of them, sometimes as active players, sometimes as shadows. There was Duane, a mysterious pre-Callie figure, who'd done drugs with my mother but she'd never tell me which ones. Kevin, who was always trying to take us on road trips to Texas to see his family. Emmett, the army man—to this day the reason we lived in Jacksonville, near the Mayport base, even though he'd been gone since I was about four.

My mother's lapses of singledom were always the briefest windows. Two or three weeks, if that. She never would have admitted it, but she needed a partner around. Somebody to complain to, to lean her head into on the couch, somebody to pick up the groceries or the mail or that week's Blockbuster. My friends never asked for stories about these moments, and my mom never offered them, but they did make up the majority of what those relationships really were: simple errands and kindnesses, all little things, like signals of compassion flashing at one another intermittently from faraway vessels.

***

Lincoln had always been hard to pin down. Not a drug addict, not an army man. I'd liked him more than the others even though he was a bit anxious, a bit unpredictable. I'd stumble out at six in the morning to grab some breakfast before the bus came and he'd already be awake, although unemployed, sitting cross-legged on the couch and flipping through some old book or a ten-year-old newspaper, or playing a board game by himself. He was strange but benign, which was how I thought of people at school sometimes, too.

Forty minutes from school, nearly an hour from home, I decided to breach the subject. "Conny?" I said.

"Mhm."

"Where are we going?"

Again the light came back into his eyes, like he'd been floating through space and just now placed himself back in the car. "Oh!

Sorry, I guess I didn't tell you," he said. He laughed nervously. "We're going to go and make some money not too far from here."

"Make some money how?"

A chill had frozen throughout me. But Lincoln reached down into the little compartment under the armrest between us, rummaged around amidst the crumpled bills and McDonald's wrappers, then came up with a Ziploc bag. Inside were a few small lumps of rock, about the size of chicken nuggets. There were even a few sparkly little rock crumbs in the crease and pinched corners of the bag.

"I don't get it," I said.

"It's gold, Callie! This is some *real genuine gold*. I found it when I was poking around my backyard the other day. Isn't that something?"

He handed me the baggie, and I turned it in my hands, peering through the plastic. The last time we'd been to see Lincoln had been maybe eight months earlier—so a few months after he and my mom had broken up, but back when they were still flirting with the idea of getting back together. Back then at least, he'd been living in one of those squat ranch-style houses you see off the edge of a highway. One level, a crumbly concrete stoop and a squashed, tangled yard. We'd driven out there and I'd waited in the car with the windows open for a humid half an hour, and then the front door had swung open and my mom had stormed out, Lincoln hollering in the doorway like a wronged kid. I wondered if he was still living there and if that backyard was the one where he'd found the gold.

"Are you sure gold is what it is?"

"Yeah. I scratched it a little, it glints really bright if you just rub the dirt off. You can try if you want."

I didn't want to open the bag. Although I'd asked it, the importance of my own question wasn't quite with me. Even if the answer were yes and it was gold, I'd still been kidnapped, hadn't I?

"So we're going—"

"My buddy knows this guy in Yulee, one of those Cash-4-Gold guys. He says he's really the real deal. I've met him a couple times but never, you know, in this context. But Jimmy, my friend, says I might have a real miracle on my hands and I shouldn't waste it at some pawn shop that wouldn't even know what it's worth."

"Oh." I tried to think if I'd met a Jimmy but couldn't remember if I had. There was a James Foley at school on the swimming team who Sam and Evana and Jessica, and I by extension, were all in love with. "So," I said to Lincoln, and I meant to be like, *Does my mom know where I am*, but the sudden irrational urge to be polite wrangled me into saying instead, "What were you doing in the backyard?"

"Oh, you know. Just poking around," he said vaguely. Then he cleared his throat roughly and sniffed, wiping his nose self-consciously with the huge sleeve of his jacket. "A funny thing happened, actually. Well, not funny, I guess. My dad sort of died. Which is fine," he added in a rush, as if I were about to fall all over him with my sympathies, "we weren't all that close. I hadn't seen him in years. But I was remembering he gave me this nice silver-rimmed compass once when I was a kid, and then one day, I guess I was about fifteen, I got so mad at him for some stupid thing that I went out to the backyard in the middle of the night and buried it. So I was seeing if I could find that compass, really."

"You really still live in the same house now you did when you were fifteen?"

"No," he said, and laughed. "No, I guess I wasn't thinking all that much at the time. You know how I can get sometimes."

He reached over and squeezed me on the shoulder, grinning slightly as if I were still his pseudo-daughter. *Were you thinking all that much at the time you picked me up from school,* I wanted to ask, *'cause I get the feeling no.*

"But hey," he said, "we got some gold out of it!"

He seemed triumphant. I nodded graciously and put the Ziploc bag back down among the fast-food wrappers.

Trees smeared by the window. The clouds had darkened, and the woods had taken on their way of looking like night in the middle of the day, swaying and ruffling. In Florida, at least the area where I live, everything looks like a place where someone might get murdered, and everything also looks beautiful.

"How's your mom?" asked Lincoln.

"She's good. She's got a boyfriend," I said, which was a lie. "His name is Alex and he's this big surfer guy." Then I added, I don't know why, "My mom is the most popular of all my friends."

Lincoln gave me a strange sidelong look.

"Well, good," he said. "I'm glad she's doing well."

"She's so happy. Like really happy."

My voice didn't sound angry, but I said it out of anger. I was angry at Lincoln for picking me up without asking my mom, for not thinking about anything ever, for putting me in the position where I had to hate him. I wanted to like him again: Conny and Callie. I hated him for taking that option away.

I tried to remain indifferent about it, but I did feel bad about Lincoln's dad dying. Lincoln really had been one of my favorites of my mom's off-and-on guys, which was why the stupidity of this car ride, this illegal reunion, got to me. I would've been fine if she had married him. He'd had a sit-down talk with me one afternoon about my dad, totally impromptu during one of our Bruster's trips. I'd been racing the summer heat to the end of a birthday cake ice cream cone, and I don't remember how but Lincoln and I had gotten to talking about my dad, who'd run out on my mom before I was born. He could be anywhere in the world, including underground, for all I knew. It was true Lincoln could be spacy sometimes, and sometimes he and my mom would yell at each other until their voices scratched, but he was really all there in that conversation, like he could tell it meant something to me. He said he knew it sucked, growing up in such an awful place and feeling like you had something missing, but that a lot of different things can be parents if you want them to be. This ice cream cone can teach you about life. This bright red bench can be there for you. He was trying to make me laugh, and it worked.

So yeah, I felt bad about his dad even though they hadn't been close, even though I'd been led astray into Lincoln's pickup. I wondered if it was too early for me to have Stockholm syndrome.

The truck slowed down, and we turned onto a gravel drive that made its metal body bump and rock. The place looked like somebody's house—only meager curtains of trees between here and the other nearby buildings—but there was a wind-beaten sign near the front door that said, CASH 4 GOLD!!! The sign was orangey-yellow with black letters, standing up on wires like an election ad.

Lincoln looked at me. "You want to stay in the car or anything? I'll understand if you don't want to meet my friend Bobby."

"No. I'll come."

He looked happy about that. We both got out and slammed our doors and walked up the drive, Lincoln holding the baggie full of gold. Before we reached the house, he said, "I'm really glad you came. I would've just gone by myself, but at the last second it occurred to me that you might think this was really cool. You've always been such a cool kid. I was holding this gold and I was just like, Callie would think this was so neat. I should show her this."

He seemed so genuine, so excited. That's me, I thought. *This is so neat.*

A big guy in a tee shirt opened the door and stared at us. He had a scruffy chin and wore extra-large faded blue jeans.

"Bobby!" said Lincoln. "Hey, how's it going?" He held up the Ziploc bag like a trophy. "I brought the gold!"

Bobby squinted, even though it was five in the evening and dark out. The trees rustled and whispered at my and Lincoln's backs, warm and blurry-gray.

"I thought you were kidding," he said.

"No, man, look. Here."

Bobby barely glanced at the lumps in the bag. "Man, I don't think that's…"

"It *is*," Lincoln insisted. "C'mon, just look at it. Just really quick, we came all the way here."

Bobby looked from Lincoln to me. He didn't ask who I was, if I was Lincoln's daughter. He just sighed.

Inside, Bobby humored us at a big wooden counter plastered with flyers. The little room contained two or three aisles of pawn junk and precious metal accoutrements: silver necklaces and watches, a bunch of identical white coffee mugs, some embroidery. Bobby handled Lincoln's findings carefully and poked them with little metal instruments, like what dentists use to scratch at your teeth, and examined them through a big magnifying glass.

Lincoln and I waited for the *wow* moment. The, *Oh my God, you've done it—you've really done it!*

Instead, Bobby leaned back with a big stretch and put down the magnifying glass. "It's not gold."

Lincoln didn't get it right away. "Is it *anything*?" he asked anxiously.

Bobby shook his head, glaring. "It's not anything. Anyone with two working eyes can see it's not anything. Now can you buy something or get out?"

Lincoln looked at me sadly, like he wanted me to tell him what to do. Like that was my job. "Callie? You want anything?"

"No."

"I could get you one of those necklaces."

"I don't want those."

"All right." He sighed. I had pictured him exploding like he did that last time with my mom, screaming and jabbing his finger into the air. Instead, he clapped Bobby on his broad shoulder. "Sorry to waste your time, man."

The first drops of rain were falling when we went back outside, leaving dark spots on my tee shirt. Trees crowded in over the driveway. Lincoln and I got back in the truck and turned onto the main road, heading back the way we'd come.

"Sorry to waste your time, too, Callie," he told me, shaking his head. His voice sounded strangled. "I really just thought you'd think that was really cool."

"Can I have that?" I asked. He was still clutching the Ziploc bag, white-knuckled, over the steering wheel.

He looked startled. "You want it?"

"I guess."

"It's not gold apparently."

"Whatever."

He handed it to me. I didn't even look at it, just held it in my lap.

"Lincoln," I said gravely. It was time. "Does my mom know you picked me up today?"

Lincoln blinked. He kept watching the road, but a glaze had come over his eyes as if the question confused him. Then a crease appeared in his forehead and his face moved in on itself a little, crumpling like a napkin. "Man. I just wanted to show you the gold I found. That's all—"

"So she doesn't know?"

"I just wasn't thinking. I wasn't thinking." As though struck with a new thought, he turned to glance at me. "Shit. I hope I didn't scare you, Callie. I would never've meant to—"

"You didn't," I assured him. "You're fine."

"Your mother was right. I really just never think. I'll take you back to her right now, Callie," he promised me. "Straight away."

I nodded. I could tell he felt bad. But my anger and indignation were ebbing away, now, into pity, which felt somehow even worse. I pressed my cheek to the window and watched the sky going by over the marshes and the distant dark trees, the rain rippling through the tall grass. I wondered where Lincoln would go after he dropped me off. Back to Smoothie King or some other strip-mall job, back to his empty house with the dug-up yard—what *was* it, I wondered, if it wasn't gold?

Before we got all the way home, before we'd even gotten back into the city, sirens came on in the distance behind us. The lights blurred together in the rain pelting the back windshield, blue and bright red.

Lincoln and I looked at each other. He was already pulling over. This wasn't going to be one of those stories where we ignored the authority and rigidity of the world as if they could never touch us and just drove off into the sunset together, and Lincoln could be my new dad or whatever and we'd both have at least one real friend in the world.

"I didn't mean to scare you," Lincoln said again.

"You're fine."

"I just thought we'd have some fun together like we used to."

"I know."

It was 5:15. How far from home was that? I didn't know, didn't care. I folded the Ziploc bag and slipped it into my pocket while Lincoln parked on the shoulder and shut off the engine. Knowing I'd vouch for him and it wouldn't matter, and I'd get home and there'd be a certain amount of screaming that night and maybe crying and hugging and then I would go to sleep and wake up the next day. Knowing this was the type of story where I'd never see Lincoln again. I leaned back into the seat that smelled like his jacket and watched the thunderous rain slamming the grass and the windshield, suddenly very patient, knowing the story was already over and that I would be okay no matter what.

Natural Fit

Let's meet our heroine. She is a column of dust spiraling across the desert; her parents are wind and soil.

She bears us no ill will. She has ex-boyfriends and ex-girlfriends like you and me: the jagged pillar that split into a stalactite and a stalagmite when she told him she couldn't do long-distance anymore, the cloud that clenched into a gray fist when she kicked her out. Her first real love was a floe of Arctic ice, spun through with fractals like the geometry that makes up sugar. Beautiful. No one—especially not a spine of dust, dry and sun-scorched—could look at those mazes of cool frost and not feel drawn into something. They'd understood things about each other no one else did: the assembled, granular work it took to feel composed, the extremity of a stripped wind. The last time she'd seen that tablet, they'd been floating away from her, chilling the water around them, saying, *I'm finding our children. I'm taking them to my mother's house.*

She loves all her exes. She's dust, already old the day she was born. But they each made her feel new in their own ways. They all had good forms, lived in a way she found beautiful. Each time they split, it was natural.

A column of dust has room for power but not for hate. She would better be spent with the wind on rainy days, feeling herself soften, darken, and then flicker back up, alight, when the sun settles into her as far as it can. Exhaustion can become a kind of transformation, and few know this feeling as closely as dust. Maybe she's not the best heroine, except that on some days it feels like the world has changed without telling her and is conspiring against her, also without telling her. This can be a good enough reason to root for dust.

She fell in love with a root once. It was hard for them to speak to each other because the root was underground. To speak with her love and see their face, she lay herself along the grassy dirt and waited for rain. The elements guided her down over a hundred years, working with her, deeper, closer. Her arrivals always take this kind of time and heart, more magic than the world can immediately recognize. But she does this kind of thing for her loves. Like all of us, she wants to find a natural fit.

When she found the root, she rested there for a night, neither of them saying anything. When they could both feel the morning trickling down through the soil, clearing through the worm paths and vessels of ferns and fungi, the root whispered, as kindly as they could, *I don't think this is working*. Knowing they'd have to wait for their beloved all over again, if it took a hundred years or more. Our heroine whispered back, *I know*. It was painful—how many times can one do this? All for one night. Maybe it was like people said—more about the journey. She gathered herself up and kissed the root once in the way dust kisses, which carries all her tenderness and hidden powers, all her personal history and her care. She went out the same way she came in, a fierce down and a nameless, excruciating up.

But she's still out there now: brush in her wake. Sun glinting in her particles.

You could've driven past her. She's bending through tree limbs; she's paying attention. She still remembers on some molecular level what it was like to be a star. There goes one of the things she loves now.

Revenge on Meter Street

When the haunting came back, Jules and I were four years divorced, the house a divide between us too sprawling to bridge. Over the course of the spiraling months we'd lived there, I would climb into the attic and find her kneeling in the corner, motionless in shadows, dark hair pooling across her back. She'd roll over in the middle of the night and think she was holding me close, and then the real me would come back into the room from the hallway, bathroom light flicking off behind my silhouette, and whatever was in her arms would vanish. Chairs and family heirlooms would be not where we left them. There were a few worse things, too.

The people in our neighborhood didn't like us anyway. So we went and stayed with friends for nearly two months while we figured things out, tried getting the house back on the market. A weird interim of long nights trying to fall asleep on friends' couches, staring at unfamiliar ceilings for hours with strained eyes, often padding away from one another around one or two A.M. to hide in aching bathrooms full of the lotions and towels and hair strands and smooth soaps of happier people. A period of time I barely remember now. The move was maybe a bad decision—we spent literally all our money—but we got out.

I still had nightmares about it long afterward, although that's probably neither here nor there. After I had not seen Jules in four years, she showed up at my door, and brought it all back with her.

***

I opened the door to my rowhouse still in my bunny-ear slippers, and that was where Jules's eyes went first. "Oh my god, Carrie," she said, looking down, an involuntary smile curling across her face. Instantly I wanted to slam the door shut. What right did she have to be smiling?

Also, what right did she have to be here? I'd survived loving her once, and it had nearly killed both of us. Hadn't we proven ourselves? Could she not just be gone?

Then, so quick it could've drawn blood, she looked up at me, her lips tightening into a line. "We need to go back to Meter Street."

A noise like a laugh came out through my nose, but I didn't smile. "What?"

"Can I come in?"

In another life she would've pushed past me, would've already been inside before thinking to ask it. But she waited on the stoop, precarious—she was self-aware enough for that, at least—the summer morning settling into cloudy contrasts across the city behind her. The line of trees across the street was dotted with green and copper and gold-tinged leaves, like a long-abandoned coin collection.

I stood aside and let her in.

She strode past me, started rifling through my closets and pantry as though she'd been here before. "I'm sorry to intrude," she said while opening and closing all the doors in my kitchen, bending to peer inside cluttered cupboards. "I know this probably isn't an easy way to start your day." She glanced over at me sidelong and took in my pajamas: baggy sweatpants, bunny slippers, and a faded green tee shirt that read QUENCH YOUR SUMMER THIRST over a cartoon of a Ken-looking man drinking beer while riding a surfboard.

"It's Sunday," I said, defensively. "And I wasn't expecting anyone." Annoyed, I followed her around the kitchen island. She'd found the stash of tealight candles in the drawer by my sink and started collecting them all in a steel mixing bowl, of all receptacles, along with the Morton salt from my pantry. "Are you robbing me?"

She flipped her dark hair back, away from her face. She'd cut it to her shoulders since the last time I'd seen her, signing papers at her attorney's office four years earlier. It made her look like a different person, and her bony face—once sharp and gaunt, and sickly-pale, like a girl from a Tim Burton movie—was now steeled and young.

It occurred to me, a little abstractly, that she was attractive—in the way I'd first been attracted to her, way back when we were both practically kids. Back when I looked at her and all I saw was *pretty* and *mysterious* and *strong*, all melding together with beautiful specifics that multiplied and strengthened with each new thing I learned about her. It felt dissonant getting a glimpse of that now, being hit with the very basic and obvious reminder that all these years, I'd been remembering her at her worst.

"Someone new moved in," she said. "She tracked down my number through the realtor. She sounded really freaked out on the phone—"

"Oh, Jules—come on, that doesn't mean *we* have to—"

"She said she's hearing noises from the attic." Jules raised her eyebrows at me and wiggled them a couple times for effect. "And rattling sounds from her windows at night."

"Good...for her..."

Most people are lucky to survive one truly horrifying experience in their lives. Just having Jules standing in front of me was plenty of a visceral reminder for me without returning to the house itself—it brought me back to our early days after moving out, when I couldn't even look at her without seeing a flash of what she'd become: a haggard figure levitating in the kitchen at 3:00 A.M., neck bent and long black hair hanging. Almost not even a person. To say nothing of what I'd become.

"We have to help her." Jules hefted the mixing bowl up against her hip. "I know things got—weird between us, after. And I'm sorry for coming here and throwing this all at you at once. But this girl's really young, she's scared, and she's all by herself. I'm going to help her either way, and I'd—" She sucked in air, and for the first time her dark eyes flickered away from mine, with something near irritation. "I'd rather not do it alone. And you—"

I twisted my head to the side in an almost-nod, grudging. My toes curled inside the bunny slippers over the tile kitchen floor. I knew what she meant—although we'd come eventually to hate each other, although we'd forced each other's physical presences away with almost obscene determination the last few years, I *was* the only one who'd believe her. I was the only one who'd know how she felt.

"Sure," I said, through my back teeth.

"You help people," said Jules. "You've always been so good about helping other people."

A slash of old resentment currented through me. I'd been waiting for it to hit, and now it did. That was always Jules's old refrain—how much I helped people. I was a technical writer, focused on grants and project proposals for nonprofit clients. But there was always a grain of envy seeded in me—or, no, a grain of a wish that sometimes showed itself like envy—a wish that I could write creative work. Bestsellers. The sort of thing Jules wrote. Every so often, my ego would get the better of me, through no fault of hers, and I'd complain about my frustration—but then her refrain to soothe me would always stress how much good I was doing, how many people I was helping.

If anything, this only got worse after the chaos on Meter Street. She doubled down on her assuaging, as if my hate were something that could be soothed with gentleness. As though either one of us could ever forget. Once I flung one of Jules's romance paperbacks at the wall of our new rental place and shouted how it was so easy, everything was so easy for her to say.

Maybe it was the memory of this that spurred me out of the kitchen and stalking back to my bedroom. "Fine!" I shouted over my shoulder. "Fine, fine, fine, fine, fine."

"That's the spirit!"

I thought, *Don't talk to me about spirits*, as I scrambled through my turned-out dresser drawers for a change of clothes. I kicked off the slippers and tugged on a clean-ish pair of jeans and a Washtenaw Community College sweatshirt, trying not to wonder what Jules was doing out there in the living room of my current place. Pacing around, maybe, looking for framed pictures and new books, trying to piece together the accumulated clues of my life without her. I had no serious girlfriend or boyfriend; there was nothing of consequence, really, for her to find. It was my sixth city address in the last four years, and I shrugged off more possessions with every move, whittling my life down to its bare essentials. No art on the walls. When I came back out, she was standing by the entry still in her coat, looking right at me with her head cocked and her eyes soft.

I jerked my head at the mixing bowl. "What do you need with all that?"

"It's for our exorcism," she said. "I already picked up some holy water this morning, at church."

I snorted. Four years earlier, she'd been the one going on about how she was afraid of me, of us, of our future and what might be hiding in it. Now here she was, animated and full, as if that could wipe my memory of the emptied-out shell of her.

"I didn't know you could just *pick up* holy water," I said.

"I'm Christian now."

"Oh." I couldn't tell whether she expected me to make something of this. "Well, still," I went on, "you can pick up holy water but you can't pick up candles and salt—"

"I knew I was coming here anyway. To get you." Doubt flickered across her face then, which was oddly gratifying. "Which thank you," she added. "Really."

I averted my eyes, grabbing my jacket off the rack. "Sure."

She gave an apologetic smile and opened the door to the world outside, just as a fall wind gusted a cloak of leaves off the trees below and into the air, twirling above the street in raucous silence before falling.

***

I never wondered if we imagined any of it. We simply didn't. There was an evil presence on

Meter Street, and it closed in on our house and surrounded it. It choked the shutters and tightened against the chimney and the front door, it groaned in the crawlspace beneath the porch and blacked out our windows.

It started with our senses, conspiring sounds we couldn't track. Then visions. Jules, home all day writing, got the worst of it. She'd say, *I think people are looking in at me through the windows.*

I'd ask, *children?*

She'd say no. *I think it's our neighbors.*

Our neighbors on both sides were elderly, could barely walk for more than a half hour at a time—but they squatted like children below the windows of our porch, whispers clamoring just out of sight, peering in with wrinkled gazes.

Then the scuttling in the walls and under the floorboards, the day I said, *I think mice are getting in.* But other days I thought they were birds. Other days squirrels, or possums, or things even bigger.

I'd come home after long days at work and find Jules hunched over her laptop screen, hypnotized. Sometimes her cheeks were stained with tears from forgetting to blink. She'd sit in the same position for hours until her muscles seized up, swamped in the blue glow of a Word document. I'd shake her loose and shut the laptop, feed her, but the rings of light would hang in her pupils for hours afterward.

We both refused to seek help. No priests for us, no psychics or ghostbusters. There was nothing in our house, we maintained to ourselves silently, independently, that needed to be exorcized.

To make peace with what was outside of our house if not what was within it, we invited our neighbors over for a housewarming party. About half came, wearing nice clothes, remarking politely on our furniture and our family photos. One of the women asked us at one point, So, *do either of you have kids?* and Jules said, *We're actually together, and no, we haven't really thought about it yet,* and the woman made a guttural *mmm* noise. *You know,* one of the other women chimed in, *I think that's great. I think it would be nice if we were all a little more open. There was actually a time in college, just once, when I kind of—well,* she finished, her smile growing nervously as she noticed all her friends' eyes on her, *it feels funny to talk about it now.*

Later, after they'd all filed out, Jules and I stumbled over each other, cracking up. Jules howled with laughter, gripped my shoulder.

It felt like we'd healed for a moment, banished whatever blasphemy lived there. Three nights later was when it locked us in. Jules was everywhere—or something that looked like Jules was everywhere. Face always hidden. Limbs splayed, edges crooking around far-off corners. *We'll get through this,* I kept saying, but I was crying while I was saying it, backing barefoot across the kitchen floor away from her, wondering if I could get to the front door and out of it. *We'll get through this together.*

***

The Chicago skyline skidded back out the window of Jules's Camry. Fall leaves stacked up to replace the gray buildings, dotting our way down Lake Shore Drive while the enormous stretch of the lake glittered beside us. Meter Street was in a suburb, a good half hour from the city, closer to the small nowhere-towns of Illinois where Jules had grown up and I'd moved after college.

"I'm surprised I found you," said Jules. "You moved, right? I saw on Facebook."

I didn't want to talk about this, because I knew what she was going to say—what I might've said, if I were her. But I nodded. "I had some trouble with my old place. Plumbing issues."

"Was that the place near Grant Park?"

I wondered if she was fishing—if she knew how many times I'd moved from some mutual acquaintance or had pieced together clues from social media. I resolved to keep my cards close to my chest, to give her only whatever details she asked for. *Only anything she wants*, I thought, the pinnacle of restraint, *nothing more.*

"No," I said. "I had to leave that place a while back. There was something living in the wall, and the landlord was being an asshole about it."

A lot of the reasons I'd left places over the past few years, I knew, were technically fixable problems. A leak in the pipes, layers of dirt that wouldn't go away, slanting and rotted floors, ant infestations. One apartment had been strangely chilly all the time, and when I left, I gave an excuse about the utilities being too high. I still saw my moves as reasonable. Meter Street had gifted me plenty of new fears, and any small kernel of something like that experience was to be avoided. I wasn't going to be that person who ignores all the signs, the creaking in the stairs and the flickering power outages, until it's too late. It was simply not worth it. Instead, I'd evolved in the opposite direction, into a person who refused to suffer a single warning sign at all.

Luckily, Jules didn't press me further. She didn't force any conversation as she steered us down the highway, toward the evil cluster of roads our younger selves had run from.

We'd moved in only a month before our wedding, and we were both in too good of moods—and too new to the world of horrors and hauntings—to heed the things about the neighborhood that had felt eerie to us even then. The realtor had done that classic scary-movie thing where he'd told us our house was the only one that ever went on the market on Meter Street, a good reason to act fast—that property saw turnover every few years or so, nothing too irregular, but all our neighbors and their families had lived in their houses since the 1950s or earlier. It was a historic neighborhood, full of legacies. The houses weren't mansions—they were middle-of-the-road, two-story affairs, but imbued with the careful preservation of decades. Families who handed down their traditions and relationships and feuds with one another like fragile heirlooms. Wood stained over the years into the idea of elegance.

But there was something about the street that made the skin of my arms prickle the first time we drove down it, and I felt it again now as Jules and I exited the highway.

The first houses started rolling up with their flat driveways like waiting tongues, their starched sidewalks and trimmed lawns and closed garage doors. We tried to reconcile ourselves to this feeling when we lived in the neighborhood, going for long runs and striking up chats with neighbors, but each interaction only left us feeling even less grounded than before. We'd go for walks and lose ourselves in hidden miles of curving, winding gray, turns and forks steering us away from our own front door in roundabout ways, the flat blue sky pressing down until it hunched upon our backs. We'd try saying hi to our neighbors, and they'd take too long to recognize us, or they'd offer a smile but we wouldn't see any teeth inside.

It was this outer world, we became convinced, that was morphing somehow and becoming a danger, becoming evil. It was the neighborhood that was troubled. Not us. We took note of every scrap of strangeness as we made small talk with our neighbors and pretended to smile, keeping track of their slip-ups in our heads to tell each other about them later. Every time somebody smiled with their skin pinched in strange places, as if they were wearing a mask. Every time we met a dog that stood still when we tried to greet it, simply watching us, tail pointed.

***

The girl's name was Charm. She opened the door of our old house wearing an oversized T-shirt, her brown hair tied back in a loose, thin ponytail. She was eighteen, Jules had told me on the way over: almost young enough to be our daughter, in another world. Her uncle was the property manager, and he was letting her stay here for super cheap to get some space from her parents, as long as she didn't move too much of her stuff in and kept it looking clean for showings ("Yeah," Jules had admitted, "I thought that sounded weird, too").

I'd known she was young, but maybe I'd forgotten what eighteen-year-olds looked like, because she looked like a child to me.

"Thanks so much for coming," she said, her eyes wide and beckoning as she waved us in.

The place looked the same. Eerily the same—the door, when Charm leaned back holding it open, cracked wide at the same angle I'd left it ajar that last night. Running for the car across the same yard—the grass the same tangled, overrun disgrace against the cropped lawns of the rest of the neighborhood. Jules and I walked in, and the floor voiced the same protests against us, the shadows of the immediate staircase and its banister and the hall table just ahead all falling along their same angles.

Jules was different, with her cut hair and flushed cheeks. My life alone, a neatly contained mess of mobility, was different now than it had been. But this house was the same, like it had frozen in time and awaited us.

"This means a lot," said Charm. Her big T-shirt was checkered with baby colors, pale pink and sky blue. "I don't know what I would've done otherwise."

"Well, I don't know how much we'll be able to help," said Jules, hugging the mixing bowl in front of her stomach.

"Just listening, that's already helping. You don't even know how much. Just believing me helps." She shook her head, flipped her ponytail back over one shoulder. "My uncle barely even picks up my calls anymore."

Jules and I glanced at each other. Charm closed the heavy door behind us.

We were never believed, never helped. We never tried to be.

I said to Charm, "Take us around. Show us everything."

***

Moving around the old house, I kept wanting to turn and ask Jules: Where have you been? I wanted it to be nice and easy for us to give answers to each other. That was the first feeling of falling in love I can remember having in life: the feeling of genuine, urgent curiosity about another person, the feeling that says, *There's so much I want to ask you, I don't know where to start, I just know I want to start somewhere, and then try to keep going.*

I didn't want her to be doing badly. I knew some sparse details about her life already, from social media and word of mouth, from what I'd imagined. But I wanted to hear it from her, her version of what mattered.

She could say:

That first year without you, I traveled and wrote you long letters I thought about sending, then burned ceremoniously. I had fever-hot nightmares, but it was okay. I was away, and it couldn't get me.

The second year, I moved back to Chicago and started therapy. I hope you've done this, too. I reconnected with old friends. My mom still wasn't talking to me, even though we were broken up now like she'd wanted. Still, I found some good things in my life. I got good at cooking without you around. I made lots of curries, chickpeas and rice.

The third year, I fell in love. I didn't think I ever could again. I walked around all year feeling stretched, in a good way. I felt like a tree, grown over the course of years to its capacity. At night if I woke up he'd be there and hold me, but I never told him about Meter Street. I told myself it was because I never got a chance. When spring came, he told me through tears that he was sorry and flew back to Austin to be with his first wife.

This year, I've mostly been writing. I needed a break. But enough months have passed, and now I guess I feel like being a hero.

***

"This is where I woke up from my nightmare last week," Charm said, pointing to the velvet curtains in the corner of the living room. They looked too long for the walls and piled up in heavy exhaustion on the wood floor. "I never sleepwalked before I came here."

She had that teenager way of shuffling around, of not quite wanting to look invested even though she was the one who'd summoned us here to begin with. The living room, still full of the antique furniture the place had come with when we'd moved in, was scattered with her school things: binders and textbooks stacked beside and atop the coffee table, a backpack leaning against the leg of the plush green armchair.

"You pay for this place yourself?" I asked.

"Yeah," she said first, quickly. Then, moving back into the hallway, she lifted one shoulder and dropped it in an awkward shrug. "I mean, kind of. My uncle's not charging me much."

"Why don't you move?" asked Jules.

"I'm not going home," said Charm firmly. "My brother's turned into some kind of YouTube asshole, and my parents are disasters. It's been a bad year." She thumbed the wall absently as she passed it. Her back was still to us as she glided down the hall, guiding us past our own old rooms. "But other than there, nowhere's cheaper than this."

"Your parents don't mind you living here, all by yourself?" I asked. "Can't you get in some kind of trouble?"

"They don't mind. They're not too far, they check in on me sometimes."

Jules and I exchanged another glance. Both of us were curious, but both of us, it seemed then, decided not to intrude on this girl's life any more than we had to.

"In here," said Charm, swinging open the door of a closet, "I thought I saw this shape the other night, under the bottoms of the coats. I nearly had a heart attack. I could see its eyes. I ran off down the hall, but it didn't chase me, and when I came back it wasn't there anymore." Jules and I had just peered inside, our shoulders nearly touching in the narrow hall, when Charm jerked away. "Oh! And here, down the hall—this is where I thought I saw hands up against all the windows—"

She hurried off, and both of us paused in the hall, looking after her. She'd gone into the kitchen.

My eyes met Jules's in the dimness. I didn't know who ought to feel guiltier: me, for what the thought of the kitchen brought back, or her for dragging us both back here to begin with. I didn't know why guilt even felt like the point, but it did.

"Come on," Charm's voice sailed down the hallway, "you have to see, this is the weirdest part—"

I started walking, but Jules grasped my sleeve, so suddenly that I flinched. "Wait," she whispered. She was frowning, and for the first time I noticed a small silver cross hanging from her neck. "What if Charm—"

"What?"

"You know..." She didn't seem able to finish the thought, at least out loud.

Yet still, even after years apart, I knew what she was thinking. "Don't worry," I whispered back. "If anyone here is a ghost of this place's past, it's us." I meant for it to be a joke, but once the words were out, I half-believed them.

"What if it's a trap?"

I searched her eyes for a moment and found the old fear. It had always been there. I tugged my arm gently away. "We knew that going in," I said. I turned and kept walking down the hall, and she followed. Better to be with me than alone.

I didn't know why I trusted Charm this far, except that some things in life really are just innocent. I really wanted that to be that—even now, even still. If Meter Street reminded me of anything, it was that you can't think everything you don't recognize is a trap. You doom yourself that way.

So many times, in these rooms and hallways, I hadn't recognized Jules. But that didn't mean what I'd seen wasn't her.

In the kitchen, Charm was waiting by the knife-rack. A new knife-rack, of course, but still in the same place: beside the stove, near where I'd been standing that night.

"They were all around," said Charm. "I was making popcorn late at night, and I looked up and saw all these hands pressing against the windows."

For a moment, I could see them. All that faceless skin, heralding nothing but hunger and fear. I thought of what Jules had said about the old people watching her, crouching like children below the flowerpots and then vanishing. I blinked, and the palms spanning the windows were gone.

It struck me how readily Charm shared these stories, stories that would have made others—would have made me, in another life—call her irrational. She already had more power than she realized, just by naming them.

"We'll stay with you," Jules said firmly. Her wide gaze flickered over to me and then back to Charm. "We don't know a fucking thing about ghosts or demons or any of that, but we brought some candles and some holy water and I figured we'd at least see what we can come up with. Together. How does that sound?"

Jules, bending low into her knees, locks of dark hair hanging together damp with salty tears and spit, muttering in an almost alien whine: *If I stay in this house another night I'll die, Carrie, I just know I will I'll die.*

"Okay." I had to force the word out. My mouth dry as an un-rained-on grave. "Okay. Yeah. Sounds good."

I stalked back down the hallway alone to grab the mixing bowl. When I came back, Jules met me just past the kitchen threshold, a look of concern on her face.

"Hey," she said. "We don't have to do this, you know. I mean, you don't have to do this."

I wanted to say, Yes, I *do*. But instead I asked, "Why are *you* doing it?"

She took a moment and leaned into the yellowing wallpaper, then seemed to think better of it, as though she wanted as little physical contact as possible with the walls which one night she'd spent crawling across like a human spider. She straightened and took on a look of solemnity. "Carrie," she said, "it's still in me. It's always in me. I see it in the mirror."

She was silent then for a very long moment, but I was afraid to ask what she meant by this.

She shook her head. "Whatever that is, whatever this place did to me—it's still in me. I need to get it out."

I let my gaze wander, away from Jules and to the kitchen behind her. I swallowed. "All right," I said. "Me, too."

We went back in.

For the exorcism, we struck up the candles and sat around the tile floor of the kitchen in a loose triangle. Jules wanted to sprinkle the Morton salt everywhere Charm had experienced a "haunting incident," but Charm said she wasn't cleaning up that much salt and if it was really such an important step, we could just scatter it around our bodies, because the things that had happened had happened to us, not to those rooms. So we sat there in our grainy salt rings while Jules brought out her holy water, which it turned out she'd transported in a Vitamin Water bottle like a kid trying to smuggle vodka. She divided the water into a few glasses that the three of us could keep at the ready, then asked us if we knew any incantations.

"Why would I know any incantations?" asked Charm.

"I don't know. This is as far as I got on the WikiHow page. I figured maybe we would get here and you might—know some?"

"Well, I don't."

I cleared my throat and said a couple of lines from *The Exorcist*. It was an earnest suggestion, but Jules looked as though I was failing to take something seriously.

As we waited for some sort of demon to arrive, our conversation took a few turns and lurches, until we started talking more about Charm and her life than about the haunting. We were curious. There were details we could feel her skirting away from about her family, even some of the specifics of her friends, like their names—maybe a just-in-case thing, a don't-talk-to-strangers instinct left over from a recent childhood. But we gathered that she was applying to colleges, undecided on a major but she was thinking about doing something with anthropology or maybe archaeology. As the day went on and the sun waned in the dusty windows, Charm offered us a meal as thanks, bringing out a crate of beer she said belonged to her uncle and making three open-faced veggie sandwiches on the stove. We forgot the holy water so thoroughly that at one point Jules accidentally drank a little of hers.

    Later, three beers in, I still didn't feel tipsy. Maybe it was the tension built up in me, or the autumn cold seeping in through the house's poor heating system, keeping me sharp.

    We kept talking and listening, playing games, waiting for the old house to fall apart. We didn't need reassurance that its sounds had been real. We just wanted it to fight us now, to see us as worthy opponents. We fell asleep with our salt circles smudged around us, white grains in the folds of our clothes, our glasses of holy water going stale where they stood.

    When I woke up, it was two or three in the morning and Jules was bending over next to me, passing her hand back and forth over a tealight candle to create flickers.

"Wake up. I have a question for you." When I didn't stir, something lukewarm flicked my face, and I looked up and saw her holding her glass of holy water.

I willed myself to mumble, "That's holy."

"I want to know what you think about something."

I sat up groggily from the pillow I'd made of my sweatshirt atop the hardwood, and whispered, "What?"

"Sometimes I wonder—don't you?—whether I died? Or whether maybe we both died, that last night we were in here?"

I could feel myself still blinking, still fighting to rise all the way to the surface of consciousness. I glanced over at the body lying nearest me: Charm, on her stomach, cheek pressed into the floor and mouth open.

"I don't know, maybe? No," I said. I tried bringing the details of my real apartment into sharper focus, the office where I worked. "No."

"Come over here."

It was very dark, and the digital clock on the oven read 2:55 in the morning. I couldn't quite make out her eyes.

"No," I said.

"Come over here. Where we can talk louder."

Her hair hung long. I frowned at her, then propped myself over on my elbow and noticed the real Jules, across from me on the floor, slumped with the rising and falling of sleep.

"Oh, wow," I mumbled, my heart kicking up, "all right, fuck off—"

The not-Jules arced, spine twisting up and over like a cat's. She slammed both hands into the floor in agitation, fingernails digging the hardwood into shavings. When she looked up at me her eyes glowed and her teeth were sharp, her mouth moving strangely as if to keep something inside it.

"Jules," I said loudly. Then I shouted it, louder and louder until she woke up. "Jules! JULES!"

Her eyes opened in a jolt, two tiny shines in the dark room, as suddenly as if from a nightmare. Or maybe she was waking into one. I still wasn't sure I wasn't dreaming myself.

As soon as she woke, the room quieted.

But I could still feel the other Jules watching me from some corner. Could feel all the hidden presences and evils and eyes of the place watching me, the way I always can.

I reached one hand out across the cold floor, then the other, lying on my stomach. Wordlessly, she reached back. Her shoulders were stiff now and her eyes bright with terror. I wondered if she could see everything that I could, feel everything hiding from us in that room. Some of it, probably—and then there were probably some things that she saw and I didn't, and would never have wanted to. The ends of Jules's fingers clasped mine, and we held onto each other in the darkness.

Clutching her fingers, looking into her eyes, I thought for the first time in a while not about how frightening it had been for me, seeing her and not knowing what I was looking at, but about how it must have been for her too. Those hours at home with it, during the day when I wasn't there; the times when it would take hold of her. Where had the real her gone, in those moments? She didn't know how to tell me, just like I didn't know how to tell her how hard I'd clutched the sheets back when I had to fall asleep in the same bed as her.

A memory switched back on in my head at this thought, one that had remained locked from me for a long time. On a few of those nights, waiting for what was to come, Jules and I had gone to sleep gripping each other, holding each other as tight as vices, almost painfully, as if the thing trying to pull us apart would do it physically. Wishful thinking that if I pressed my forehead right up next to hers, looked directly into her eyes and memorized their shape and color exactly, I could prevent those eyes from flipping open in the middle of the night and glowing over me while I slept. Nighttime felt like a time when we could make these wishes—when our kindest selves could be allowed to meet, just occasionally, on a common ground, a dream plane.

***

Toward the very end of our marriage—many months after leaving Meter Street—I'd fallen apart sobbing in a coffee shop with a mutual friend of ours. Jules of course had not been literally haunted in months, but the possession had left in its place in her heart a cold emptiness, a vacant refusal to speak to me or even look at me. I wasn't tuned out; I knew where this new guardedness came from. I knew how much she'd suffered, and how much fear she still carried.

"There are still times when it's good," I'd said to my friend, trying furiously to compose myself. I'd ordered a cappuccino and then promptly let the whole thing go cold. "Sometimes if we're playing the right board game, or watching the right movie—or, I don't know. We'll have a few drinks, and then it's all—it's warm again. It's okay."

The friend had stared back at me with a sadness that I, doubter that I was, knew I did not deserve. Dissolving would have been so nice, but I could feel every molten crack of myself. My brain felt the type of misty and rigid that it always felt post-crying, only these days it felt like that all the time.

My friend did not say what we were both probably thinking, what I knew in theory but could not for the life of me seem to make myself believe: that if it takes a complex series of conditions for a person to want you, they don't want you. If for them to love you it needs to be nighttime, or you need already to be in the same bed, or they need a few drinks—it's not love. Not anymore. Not the kind I'd need, if I wanted to survive.

"You went through something terrible together," said the friend. For a moment they seemed unsure of where to proceed from there; then they reached out with both of their calm hands and covered mine. "You don't have to do it over and over again."

***

Jules knit her hand inside mine, and we guided one another from hall to hall. We kept hold of each other's hands, not out of love but at least out of a feeling of needing to be together. We walked soundlessly up and down hallways, stepping in and out of rooms. Where shadows pooled, we walked up and stood in them, let their impersonal chills pass over us. We gazed into mirrors with the lights off until we found ourselves in them and knew it was us. Our hearts beat loud enough to hear them in each other's chests. We pressed our free hands to the windows and left smudges and prints for the night outside to witness: proof we were there.

I thought about what we might tell Charm in the morning. Not to make this place her adulthood, maybe. Fear gets old fast. It didn't feel like our place to tell her to leave, when we didn't know what she would be going back to; maybe I'd ask Jules if she wanted to get something for breakfast, and maybe we could see if Charm wanted to come along. Just for the morning, just for a meal. All I knew was that this wasn't any kind of place to be all alone.

The uneasiness never left; it never felt like Jules and I defeated anything. We wanted to be in this together, but I couldn't hear what was in her head, and she couldn't see what I saw through my eyes, because we were two different people. Walking around the same places together, seeing and hearing the same things at the same time: This was all we could do. Whatever we wanted, this was as close to one another as we could be.

Ophelia's Birthday

One of the boys' names was Jesse James, no relation, and the other's was Robert Ford, also no relation. They were just two twenty-first-century boys, fifteen and sixteen, who happened to be named Jesse James and Robert Ford respectively—but by then, both of them had seen stranger things in this life.

They'd been asked today to pick up Jesse James's cousin from Dave and Buster's. Her name was Ophelia (James) and it was her thirteenth birthday—the first, by her own measure, to really mark her growth into adulthood. All her birthdays previously had been celebrated at the Chuck E. Cheese around the corner on Friebolt and Marks Street, where Jesse James's older brother worked and could offer them a discount. He did a lot of different jobs at Chuck E. Cheese, from collecting prize tickets to cleaning the bathrooms, and when they all went for Ophelia's birthday, he'd usually dress up as Chuck E. Cheese and bring out the cake and then, after leading everyone in the happy birthday song, take off the big mouse mask and surprise them all by being himself.

But this year, Ophelia had announced, she was thirteen. *You all know what that means*, she'd said, examining Jesse James and his mother across the card table in the kitchen, poking a spork in each of their directions. What it meant was, she was a *teenager*, a.k.a. no longer a child or at least not a Chuck-E.-Cheese-level child.

"I don't see why we've gotta go at all," said Robert Ford, hanging in the doorway by the fingertips of both hands and frowning a little. He was a tall, mousy-haired boy who hated bright lights and loud noises.

"We don't need to *stay*," said Jesse James. "She just needs a ride."

"Her parents aren't there?"

Jesse James knitted his eyebrows together and looked at Robert Ford like he should've known better than to ask. Ophelia lived at his house most of the time because her father was out of the picture, and her mother was often what Jesse James's mother liked to call "in and out of trouble." They hadn't seen her in a little bit, so he assumed she was in trouble currently.

"What about *your* mom? I mean, who threw the party?"

"She was there, duh," said Jesse James, a little annoyed and entertained at once. "But she had to drive some of the other kids home.

Ophelia called me and said she hasn't come back yet, and all the other kids have left, and she doesn't feel like waiting around any longer. And the people at Dave and Buster's won't let her leave by herself because she's only twelve. So could you just—"

"All right! All right," said Robert Ford. He mashed his feet into a couple of shoes by the door without bending down to tie the laces, snatched his dad's key ring off its hook and ambled out onto the icy stoop. He slipped a bit but kept his hand on the doorknob so he only fell partway.

"Ha!" said Jesse James.

"Shut up!" Smiling, Robert Ford pulled himself back up and yanked the door shut in the process. "That's just how I close doors in the wintertime."

"Yes," said Jesse James, skating haltingly across the driveway in his old sneakers. "As a matter of fact, this is how I walk in the wintertime—"

"You've got to become *one* with your *environment*."

"Valuable life lessons—"

They got into the warm pickup, and Jesse James hugged his knees to his chest and rubbed his hands together and smelled the good fabric truck smell while Robert Ford started the engine and turned the heat on.

Once they got out of the neighborhood, the roads weren't bad, only shiny and crunchy with salt.

Jesse James and Robert Ford, true to their names, knew they were meant to be bad boys. They couldn't remember anymore whether they'd become best friends intentionally, or if it had simply happened because everyone else kept assuming they must be. But either way, at some point, they'd developed a murky plot together: Once they were both old enough to drive legally and had gotten their high school diplomas, they were going to run off west and fulfill their family-given destinies. They'd smoke cigarettes and wear leather that smelled like cigarettes. They'd hold up trains and banks together, but—they had agreed on this point early—they'd only rob rich people. Rich *bad* people, if they could manage it. They'd be outlaws, just sort of the Robin Hood type.

They knew they'd be the perfect outlaws because they were comfortable trying anything together, which meant compared to more insecure outlaws they'd have a bit of an edge. At school they'd both joined the chess club for a little while—a very outlaw thing to do in their school's social stratosphere—to get good at strategic thinking. At lunch, back in elementary school, they'd taken turns concocting horrifying meals for each other out of cafeteria food (strawberry-milk salad; ketchup-pudding; watery chicken tenders) to build up their tolerances in case either one of them was ever forced to eat something disgusting in a strenuous train-robbing situation. Once, they'd taken some of Mrs. Ford's makeup out of her bathroom and powdered up each other's faces and put on lipstick: practice for if they ever needed a spur-of-the-moment disguise.

And very recently, they'd started practicing crime. Last weekend they'd driven Robert Ford's dad's truck to the nearest mall and stolen two silk shirts by going into the fitting rooms and putting them on under the tee shirts they'd already been wearing. Jesse James had been sweating the whole time, the fancy navy collar closing onto the bare skin of his throat in a way that felt both gentle and threatening at once. He could've sworn the sales lady was watching them as they left, her gaze buttoning itself hotly into the back of his neck.

But as soon as he'd made it into the car with Robert Ford and they could hug and scream and high-five, he'd realized the whole thing had been easy, and instantly he could breathe again.

In the car on the way to Dave and Buster's, Robert Ford watched the road and Jesse James spent the whole drive fiddling with the radio dial, trying to find a station even though the place was right around the corner and there were only two good stations in town.

"I think," said Robert Ford grandly—the way he always spoke when he started a sentence with I *think*—"I'm going to get really good at magic tricks."

"You already can do that," Jesse James said, still playing with the radio, his feet up on the glove compartment.

"I know, and I'm okay now. But I'm going to get *really* good. So we can use it in our outlaw-ery."

"Do they call it outlaw-ery? *Do* they?"

"Who is *they*?" said Robert Ford disdainfully.

"Okay," said Jesse James, and shook his head. "What kind of magic tricks?"

"Next-level kind. Like you know right now I can do card tricks," he said seriously, his eyes still scanning the strip-mall streets ahead of them. "And the coin disappearing. And the ball-under-the-cup thing."

"Right."

"It's about confidence," Robert Ford explained, as though he hadn't talked Jesse

James through these concepts a million times before, walking around town and before the morning bell rang at school. "Like anything. If you can master the suggestion that you know what you're doing, you can do magic. If you can create the *illusion*, then you can guide how people really think—"

"Robert," Jesse James whined, "*please—* "

"Okay, okay. So, now that I'm good at that—I think it's safe to say I'm good at that—I want to learn how to do the sorts of things they do in circuses. I think talking to animals would be the easiest place to start—"

"Like lions?"

"Well, yeah—in an ideal world. But I don't think there are any around here, so I'll have to start—"

"You can use our cat for practice if you want. Tina."

"That's what I was going to say! And eventually I'll work my way up to the really cool stuff. Like breathing fire and hula-hooping with fire." He started pulling off the road and into the parking lot.

"How will that help during a train robbery?"

Robert Ford glanced at him sidelong. "It's like you've never seen a movie in your life," he said, but he didn't elaborate. He shut off the engine, and the two of them got out of the truck. They wobbled across the parking lot, between the streaks of black ice and salty slush. The sky was one big slab of winter cloud.

Inside, it was dark and the colored lights from the arcade machines were ricocheting off the walls like over-sugared neon rainbows. Robert Ford hunched his shoulders and stayed close to Jesse James as they wove around the rows of stripy, chaotic carpet and elbowed politely past unhappy dads, kids clutching slushies and thwacking at machines, and moms clasping ribboned fistfuls of tickets to their chests.

They found what seemed like the front desk and asked after Ophelia.

"Hmmm," said the guy standing there, a man with very little face but big thick-lensed glasses to make up for it, who wore a maroon tee shirt and a Dave and Buster's baseball cap. "There's no little girl up here. But maybe try the gift shop."

At the gift shop, a young woman in another maroon shirt tilted her head from side to side and back again. "Yeah, I think I might've seen her earlier," she said. "Maybe try the bar."

The jangling music was beginning to grate on Jesse James already, the chimes of nearby machines colliding in off-key scrapes of sound and the bass kicking in his ribcage. This was why he hadn't wanted to come to the party to begin with. Robert Ford didn't look much better, his eyes darting around, pale cheeks lighting up with a skeletal glow under the rhythmic sweeps of different-colored lights. Jesse James found himself speed-walking over the carpet. He didn't understand why Ophelia hadn't just waited for them by the front door.

They went to the bar, their shoulders hunching up even more around all the over-twenty-one-year-olds drinking their beers and cocktails. They knew there were kids at school who'd started venturing into the realms of alcohol, but the furthest Jesse James and Robert Ford had gotten was a mostly empty scotch bottle from the liquor cabinet in Robert Ford's dad's basement: barely a sip left for each of them. Really disgusting stuff, but they knew they'd have to get used to it if they were going to be hardened criminals one day. True blue all-American heroes. At least they could help each other through it.

The zinging sound effects and exclamations of the games were a little more muffled over here, and a few of the adults glanced at them as though trying to discern how they fit in: old enough that they could have pretended to be mature, but instead here they were with their untied shoelaces, their nervous expressions and shirts with the collars stretched out. The bartender ignored them until they waved their hands in his face and told him they weren't trying to buy any drinks, they were just looking for a little girl from a birthday party.

He nodded understandingly and then shook his head. "Not here," he said. "You try the front desk?"

"Are you *sure*?" Robert Ford persisted. "She didn't ask you to use the phone? She called us from here earlier."

The bartender only looked at them blankly, like he couldn't tell what they wanted from him.

Jesse James and Robert Ford stalked back together into the disarray of games and machines, scanning every corner for Ophelia and calling her name. Jesse James tried to ignore how his heart had started beating a little faster. They walked past the machines that push golden coins slowly toward you like a promising tide that never comes all the way in, past the resounding *roll-click* of Skee Ball and the breathy levitation of the air hockey tables. Cue sticks thwacked against pool balls somewhere far off, like the distant out-of-sight gunfire that sounded in the woods near Jesse James's house during hunting season.

"Ophelia!"

"*Ophelia!*"

"Fee!"

"You know something—" Robert Ford suddenly snagged Jesse James's coat sleeve. "Maybe your mom already came back and got her. I bet that's it."

Jesse James sucked in a breath. This did make him feel a little better. "I can't just leave if I don't *know*, though," he said plaintively, and suddenly the unfairness of the situation struck him: *He* wasn't Ophelia's father, wasn't even her older brother, not technically. There was no reason he should be responsible for her—he should be able to leave right now with Robert Ford and not even feel bad about it. But because he knew Ophelia had recently needed help and because he didn't know if she still needed it, he felt he had to be the one looking after her, just in case nobody else was, which, maybe, they simply weren't. He looked desperately away from his friend and to the glass cage full of bright stuffed animals with the claw waiting to grab them, and said, "Nobody ever tells me anything!" He felt like he might be about to cry.

"Let's go back to the main desk," Robert Ford urged. "We can borrow the phone and call your house. If nobody picks up, we'll figure out a new plan—but I think that seems like the next step."

Jesse James loved how Robert Ford was always thinking of the next step. "All right," he agreed.

Maybe he should have just gone to the party. Then there wouldn't've been any danger of Ophelia getting separated from anyone—he would have been there, and they could've gone straight home. It wouldn't have been *fun*, he thought, a guilty, prickly heat settling into his forehead, but it was only for a couple hours, and it would've been the nice thing to do, the supportive thing. And after all there was nothing about Ophelia that didn't deserve to be supported.

They went back to the front desk and found not only the guy from before there, the one with the big glasses, but also the girl from the gift shop that they'd met earlier. She'd come over and was leaning with one elbow on the glass counter and talking to the front desk guy. They both turned when Jesse James and Robert Ford came over and blinked, almost in unison.

"Oh, hi," said the girl. Her name tag said RACHEL. "You guys want some prizes?"

"No," said the guy with the thick glasses. "Remember? They were looking for their little sister."

"My cousin," said Jesse James.

"That's right. Did you find her?"

"No." He thought for a second about saying, *Did you?*, but he didn't want to start an argument. "Could we use your phone?" he asked. "I want to call home and see if my mom got her."

"Yeah, 'course."

They both stepped aside so the boys could join the guy with the thick glasses behind the counter. Jesse James picked up the phone while just behind them the girl Rachel said, softly, "Um—shit, shit?" kind of like a question, and then the guy with the thick glasses' hand gripped Jesse James's arm very tightly and Robert Ford's hand flew into his like a little bird.

Jesse James turned around with the phone still against his ear to see who'd come up to the counter. A bearded man in a big coat was now standing next to Rachel with one hand stuffed in his coat pocket.

Jesse James looked at Robert Ford next to him in one last, lingering moment of puzzlement. He hadn't seen the weapon, but the understanding of it descended upon him now. All the color had left Robert Ford's face in a quick sweep. He looked at Jesse James rigidly, unmoving and unblinking, as though in this one moment of glassy eye contact he could tell Jesse James everything he had ever needed to.

"All the money in the register," the man in the big coat said. "Now. I don't wanna hurt anyone."

The world beyond these few square feet had become a blur. So many people around, and none of them looking, none of them hearing. Not the couple taking shots over at the basketball hoops, not the dad calling out somebody's name, *Amelia? Amelia?*, not the little girl who could be heard howling for someone to get her a Band-Aid, not the woman pushing the covered stroller toward the laser tag area with the hidden baby sending up screams from inside. Kids raced around a maze of lit-up corridors that now felt impossibly distant, chasing after one another and calling each other's names, shrieking when they won their games, shrieking when they lost. For a moment all Jesse James could hear were the cries of children.

And then Rachel. "You got it," she said. "Freddie, give it to him."

Freddie, his head down so far his thick glasses were slipping to the tip of his nose, was opening the register, his right hand trembling with the keys.

Jesse James felt so frozen that the plastic phone pressed to his ear had switched to feeling just like another part of his head, or his hand. He'd even stopped hearing the dial tone which had been going this whole time. But now it hit him: This was a robbery, they—*they*, Jesse James and Robert Ford and company—were being *held up*, and Rachel and Freddie probably wanted to call 911 but instead here was Jesse James, stuck, holding the phone.

The same moment he realized it, the man in the big coat seemed to realize it. He looked down at Jesse James, the fourteen-year-old boy pressed back against the wall with his mouth hanging open and the phone stuck just above his shoulder, and he furrowed his eyebrows and lifted his hand out of his coat for just a second to indicate to Jesse James the end of the gun, in case he hadn't seen it before. "Be smart, kid," he said.

Jesse James didn't even nod. All he had to do was reach over and press in those three numbers—but his head was all jumbled now, and the nine and the ones kept muddling together with his mom's phone number, which part of him still wanted to dial instead. All the same he still could just punch in 911, he *could*—except that he couldn't, never could, when there was a gun anywhere near Robert Ford or himself. Bank money was a fun prize, a rush to the head, not a real thing, yet. The coat man could take all he wanted if he'd just leave.

Freddie took out the last stack of bills and handed it across the counter to the man in the big coat. The man in the big coat took the money with his other hand and stuffed it in the pocket without the gun. He nodded at them stiffly and turned from the counter, and then a loud clueless voice rang through the air.

"Jesse! You dumbass. I've been looking all over for you."

All of them—Jesse James, Robert Ford, Rachel and Freddie and the man in the big coat—turned their heads to the side. Standing several paces away was almost-thirteen-year-old Ophelia in full laser tag gear, her chest blinking laser-light red and her feet planted, laser gun hanging at her side. A wide grin was spread across her face, and her lips and teeth—they could see even from here—had gone birthday-cake purple.

"And I *know* what you're going to say," she declared, striding across the stripy carpet toward them. "I shouldn't say *dumbass* because it's cussing. But I'm thirteen now, which means I'm almost a full-grown young woman and I can cuss as much as I want."

She walked all the way up to them and stopped right next to the man in the big coat. She wasn't even thirteen yet, not for a few days; she was twelve.

Jesse James realized only now that Robert Ford's hand was still in his. He clutched it and squeezed as tight as he could. Maybe this would be like stealing from the department store, he tried to tell himself over his heart's drumming—in just a short moment now, he'd be able to breathe again.

Ophelia and the man in the big coat looked at each other squarely for a moment.

Then the man in the big coat turned and swept away from her. He made for the front door at an almost jogging pace.

"Hey!" Ophelia called after him, which made Jesse James's arm jerk up involuntarily.

The man glanced back just once from the doorway, very quickly, and Ophelia lifted her laser gun and shot a laser at him. "Pew!" she cried. The harmless red dot wiggled across the chest of his coat, and then disappeared when she dropped the gun back down to her side, giggling.

Then he was out the door and back into the daylight, gone, running for his car.

Freddie snatched the phone out of Jesse James's hand and dialed 911. "Jesus."

"Are you kids okay?" asked Rachel, but she wasn't looking at them, she was only looking forward, into space. Her voice came out in one shaky exhale.

Robert Ford tugged Jesse James back out gently from behind the counter and pulled him into a hug. They kept hugging until Ophelia started tapping them both on their shoulders—tapping, and then hitting when they didn't respond.

"What?" she demanded. "*What?*"

They broke apart. Jesse James saw now that there were a couple of tiny red nicks in Robert Ford's hand: the half-moons of Jesse James's fingernails. Now, the realization arrived in them both, it was their moment to decide—should they tell her, Ophelia? They were only a hair older than her, but at that point in time the difference felt monumental. If they told her they'd be exposing her to the evils of the world, the evils she didn't know she'd just moments ago made eye contact with. Shouldn't they keep this knowledge withheld just a little longer, so Ophelia could stay all right?

A moment passed.

No, thought Jesse James—if the world of adulthood was an evil secret, it wasn't one he was going to be responsible for keeping. This all wasn't his mess to protect. Not him and Robert Ford. He didn't care to—Rachel, Freddie, the rest of them, they could all have it.

He looked across at Robert Ford, and he could tell instantly his friend had been thinking the same thing. "Fee," Robert Ford said, and gave a hesitant, shuddering laugh. "The craziest thing just happened."

"What?" She was practically bouncing on her heels.

Robert Ford explained it all: the man coming in, his hand in the big coat, the two boys stuck behind the counter, the robber gesturing toward the cash register. He spoke haltingly through the story like he kept expecting Jesse James to interrupt him, so they could tell the story together, the way they often would. But Jesse James just nodded along.

"No *way*," Ophelia erupted. Her eyes had gone huge, her voice low and breathy. "*That* guy? The guy I—"

"Yeah!" Robert Ford smiled.

"No *way!*"

"Yes. Way." He looked at Jesse James then with a sad bright look in his eyes and nudged his shoulder softly. "I bet this never would've happened at Chuck E. Cheese," he said.

Jesse James's lips twisted, but he couldn't smile. It was hard not to see the man in the coat still standing there, hand thrust deep in his pocket, eyes glossy and looking right at him. Hard not to feel the phone imprinting a square into his ear, to hear the blurry dial tone. Probably he would think about it a lot more later. Maybe it would fall into line with the rest of the unjustifiable images that shuffled always in Jesse James's head and through his dreams: the hitchhiker he once saw rappelling up a billboard, the girl in the pink ballgown he'd exchanged a few words with last May at a Mystery Spot tourist trap, the thing in the schoolyard dead in the grass, the brother who transformed into Chuck E. Cheese to make screaming happy kids even happier. Ophelia's mother who circled in and out of their lives like a frail, excitable ghost. The things that made no sense, made so little sense they haunted him. The only thing that fit better as time went by was the understanding that things didn't really fit almost ever.

"Where the fuck is your mom?" said Ophelia. "Let's not tell her."

"Hey!" Jesse James roused himself, speaking up finally.

"What?" said Ophelia. Her eyes were glittering.

"You know what. You can't say *fuck*."

"Fuck you!" said Ophelia. "If you tell your mom I'll tell her you two got—" But she stopped short of the words *held up*, as though that, on the other hand, she wasn't sure if she could say.

They all looked at each other. Jesse James let out a breath and felt his shoulders drop. "Let's go," he said.

They went back outside, the three of them, Ophelia still clumsy and blinking like a target in her laser tag gear. Nobody from Dave and Buster's came after her. She twirled the laser gun around on her finger, then stopped and focused on the icy ground beneath her feet while they walked across the asphalt parking lot to Robert Ford's dad's truck. The sky was still a sharp silver, slashed here and there with robin-egg blue. They all felt a little uncertain, Jesse James could tell—unsure if it was okay to feel okay just now, unsure what at all to be sure of.

Halfway there, Robert Ford slipped on the ice and landed on his tailbone. "Oww," he cried, waiting for Jesse James to offer him a hand and lift him up. Ophelia laughed again, her same old high-pitched giggle traveling up into the gray sky while Jesse James pulled his best friend to his feet, and in this motion Jesse James remembered what he was sure of. It was simple, a feeling he couldn't even put words to. Like the pockets of air Robert Ford's coins disappeared into whenever he did magic: invisible, maybe a trick, but there.

"That *hurt*," said Robert Ford. "I feel it all the way up my spine."

"I didn't know you had a spine," said Jesse James, and they kept going, grabbing at one another's sleeves for rocky balance on their way back to the car.

The Summer Haunt

When a bear's staring you down, you have several options:
1. Freeze.
2. Run and hope the bear doesn't chase you. Maybe it can be distracted?
3. Drop to the ground; pretend it's like your dad when he's in a bad mood, and maybe if you play dead, he'll leave you alone.
4. Kill the bear.

It doesn't matter how you kill it. You can shoot it. Set up a trap, look away when you hear the snap. Reach out with your bare hands and strangle it, lob a fireball in its direction, blow up the forest. Blow up the world. The bear winds up dead. That's all that matters.

***

When I was twelve, I was sent to live with my uncle for a summer in the Black Hills of South Dakota. My mother made my uncle, her younger brother by four years, buy the one-way Southwest ticket. They said they did it so I could benefit from the fresh air and learn how to be a man, but the real reason was to get me away from my father. Everyone in the house was getting on each other's nerves, but he and I particularly. I heard my mother conferring with my uncle—over the phone, late one night when she thought everyone else was sleeping—asking if there was any way he could help.

My uncle was a park ranger, responsible for trail maintenance and making sure visitors to the park were well informed about the wildlife. Wildlife swarmed in the Black Hills, far more than I was used to seeing back in Indiana. Bighorn sheep, mountain lions, bison and little pine martens and white-tailed deer. And there was a single black bear, which was only there that one summer.

Rumors had been flying around for a while that year about a bear who'd escaped the Smoky Mountains and made his way west, with reported sightings along highways and in the woods of Missouri, Nebraska and maybe Kansas, over the course of June and July. He'd slipped from the grasp of park rangers, hunters, and trackers who'd taken their turns following him north as far as the urge took them, then giving up and returning south one by one, returning home. Everyone who spotted him said he was the biggest bear they'd ever seen. Once he'd been hit by a car and limped away into the roadside hills, then turned up again a couple weeks later in the background of some hiker's photograph, miraculously, wounded but strong.

"I heard they even buried it, over in Nebraska," Paul Diver, my friend that summer, told me once in a whisper. "Shot it and dug it a grave and everything. A grave for a *bear*. And then it turned up again fifty miles away—" He lowered his voice even more. "*Covered in dirt.*"

How did people know it was the same bear? A good question. They didn't, really. It probably wasn't, but they made it the same bear, by saying it was.

Anyway, late July the bear wound up in the Black Hills. I ended up killing it, which you might have guessed by now.

***

Before Paul Diver, I had exactly one good friend, this kid named Allen who let me come over to his house and play his tabletop games. I wasn't a huge talker in real life, but as a game player I was very active. My favorites were the live role-playing and choose your own adventure games, where you have to make tough, nail-biting decisions, like:
1. You've just run into a band of trolls. Do you stay and fight them or run?
2. A stranger approaches with a hood over his face. He offers you five

hundred gold coins in exchange for the chalice you've been carrying. What do you do?
3. A drunk highwayman wanders into the local tavern and starts insulting you. Do you defend your honor, or let it go?

Allen lent me storylines for a couple of these games before I left for the summer, in case I wanted to play them with my uncle. It felt weird asking a grownup to play an adventure game, although I soon found out my uncle played video games at night through a console hooked up to his old-fashioned TV, which somehow seemed even weirder. "It's nice to have a break every once in a while," he explained to me my first night there, inviting me to join him—he didn't have a second controller, but we could take turns. *Every once in a while* for him was more or less nightly: Sinking into the couch to the kind light of the animated figures in the imagined war field, a break from the paralyzed deer and the deafening crickets, a break from the rustling grass and the little pine martens.

Daytime, during my uncle's shifts, I busied myself with short walks through the woods and the stories Allen had lent me, which after a point I started trying to invent on my own. It was maybe a week after I got to the Black Hills that Paul Diver appeared, standing in a clearing surrounded by pines, skinning a gray jay.

I stopped on the path and watched him through the trees. The sight of him gave me this weird chill: standing there not on any path, the knife glinting forward and backward in his hand.

After a moment, he looked up at me and smiled—probably happy to see another boy his age there, so far away from everything. "Hi there!" he said.

"Hi," I said. "What are you doing?"

He lifted the bird, blood on both hands. "Making dinner." He jerked his head, beckoning me over. "Wanna see?"

I felt dizzied and invigorated by the otherworldliness of the choice, like I'd landed myself in a game. *A boy lifts a bloody bird, offers you a look—*

I didn't know what else to do, so I went over, pushing my way through the lush bracken undergrowth. Once I reached the clearing, I could see him more completely: a kid almost exactly my height, wire-thin, holding the knife loosely and letting the gray feathers fall to the ground without even really looking at them. He was looking at me.

"I'm Paul Diver," he said. "My dad lives over the hill."

Which hill? I would wonder, only later. "I'm James. My uncle's a park ranger."

"It's good to see another kid out here." He was grinning. "I get so bored sometimes I think I might go crazy."

I was still looking at the bird in his hands. "Are you really going to eat that?"

"Sure am. Gonna roast it. I'm a really good fire builder," said Paul Diver. "If you help me build the fire, I'll share the meat with you. Don't worry," he said quickly, when I opened my mouth. "I'll teach you how. I'm really good at it."

"I'm not too hungry," I said.

"You will be by the time it's all ready." Then he looked at me and raised his eyebrows, raised them so high he almost looked like a cartoon. "Unless you're too fancy? You're from some big city or something, I can tell."

I wasn't really, but I didn't correct him. Since I wasn't doing anything better that day and I was going to be living there for at least a couple of months, I figured making a friend might be worthwhile.

So I helped him build a fire in the clearing. We gathered up fistfuls of sweet sassafras and prickly green briar and built a little mound, set it alight. Paul Diver finished skinning the bird as the afternoon smoke rose past the high branches of the ponderosa pines, which stood tall and thin like drawn umbrellas. I never asked him how he'd caught the bird, why he wouldn't just go home for dinner. I did ask him if it was sanitary.

"What's wrong?" he asked. "You chicken?"

"I guess," I said. "If that's what you call not wanting to get rabies."

"Relax. I've done this a bajillion times, and I'm healthy as a horse, see?" He flexed his arm to prove it. It was a pretty normal arm for a twelve-year-old, not particularly muscular, but I didn't tell him this.

"Your dad," I said. "Is he a park ranger, too?"

"Yep. Elmer Diver," said the boy without blinking. "Best park ranger there ever was. It's how come I know so much about nature even though I was never in the Boy Scouts."

He lifted his stick, impaled with a scrap of roasted jay meat, above the flames. He took a bite, then offered it to me. Before I took it, my gaze landed briefly on a few of the feathers still scattered about the ground, ash-gray and tinged with blood. I'd eaten birds in Dungeons & Dragons before, camping in a dark forest or resting at a stranger's hearth. I'd made friends with a few birds who could talk and fight. A knowledge crept into me then about Paul Diver: that I had thought the Black Hills peaceful, but this smiling violence was there all along, thrumming beneath.

But if I hesitated, it passed quickly. I ended up taking the bird. I was going to be here all summer, I wanted to shape up to the task. The two of us ate the bird together, and it left a soiled, bloody taste that lingered in my mouth all the rest of the day.

***

The next day, I was sitting on the porch of my uncle's cabin when I learned there were all sorts of myths about the gray jay. My uncle sat next to me on the step, smoking and watching the sun go down through the trees. A fan was plugged into one of the cabin's decrepit outlets, the cord trailing through the open doorway and the white blades turning in slow circles in the early evening air. My uncle spotted a bird on a far-off branch somewhere, and he told me a story he'd heard from a buddy of his—my uncle called all his friends "buddies"—about a gray jay named Wisakedjak, responsible for a flood that had destroyed the world.

"Like Noah's Ark?" I asked.

"Maybe," he said. "It's just one of those old flood stories."

I liked flood stories. I'd done a school project on the Great Flood of 1844, which had devastated Missouri back before they'd built any levees. Sometimes (although I didn't tell my uncle this) I had dreams about my house back in Indiana filling up with water during the night. It would be gentle, it wouldn't wake anybody, it would actually leave everything a lot quieter and nicer in the end. But my father would drown and maybe I'd drown, too, or maybe I'd rise with the surface of the water and bump out an open window and just float away.

"I had a buddy from Maine," said my uncle, "who said they don't hunt gray jays up there."

"Is there a law?" I asked.

He shook his head. "Just superstition. They say whatever you do to the bird will be done back to you later on."

These words returned to me all summer: with the sleep I lost, with the bear I came to know, with the feeling of Paul Diver's hand gripping my shoulder by the bone.

***

I took walks sometimes in my house in Indiana, when my parents were gone at work or late at night when they were meant to be sleeping. I'd get out of bed and pad quietly down the hallways, into and out of the basement, the hall bathroom with the yellow shower curtain, the crammed entry closet where we kept all our winter coats, the pantry. Any little pocket of space. I don't think it was anything tactical—I wasn't charting the territory, or planning an escape route. I was just seeing what there was around to see and hear when everything else was taken away: the stillness of the living room and its new cloaks of shadow, the hum of the radiator. I became an expert at treading silently, from my heels to the balls of my feet to my toes, from the outside in.

Hatred was in my house, from dawn till dusk. It was not scary so much as it was infuriating. Most days—almost all days, really—nobody touched anybody else. We went around in our own little worlds. I crouched in my room, my mom moved around and around and around the kitchen, my dad sunk into his ripped brown armchair by the screen door to the yard. There were infinite little things to which you could have ascribed these evil patterns, things that had built up over the years, but I hadn't been around for most of them and the way I saw it, most of them weren't my fault. We whiled away our time under one roof together, killing our boredom, beating it back and back with TV-watching and dish-doing and alone-in-my-room game-playing until eventually, sometime in the evening usually, there'd be a dish dropped or a door left open or a plate of food handed over too passive-aggressively, and the red violent cloud of boredom would gather itself up and solidify and land against somebody's skin. We had a sliding glass door by the little living room, obscured by thin curtains but still—if you looked outside in the golden haze around six o'clock you could see the very distant trees and the big fat sky full of clouds where someday my dad was going to fly out and accomplish all his dreams. I'm not sure what these were, although I did think about it—seeing his high school buddies again, making the big leagues? A life on his own without me? Whatever it was, it was a prison's worth of family and a hundred lazy afternoons away from him, and we all felt it. It would've been easy to say my father had no dreams, but his dreams weighed heavier on that house and on our heads than anyone else's, so I know he must have had some. The last time I took the shape of his grief, he threw a pot so fast in my direction that it left a hard mark where it hit the wall.

***

I started seeing Paul Diver more and more that summer, always in the woods and in the mountains, on the random paths we spent our days listlessly traversing. My uncle didn't care what I did all day, and it seemed like Paul

Diver's father didn't care what he did, either. We climbed trees and told each other stories. He wanted to hear what Indiana was like, because he'd never left South Dakota, but he lost interest soon enough and told me South Dakota was much better anyway.

The bear turned up around late July. The first time I saw it I was by myself, chopping wood behind my uncle's cabin. It was standing on all fours, facing me directly and watching me through the trees. The biggest animal I'd ever seen.

I thought about telling Paul Diver the next day—I was sure he'd heard the rumors that summer, fresh folk stories about a bear making its way west from Kentucky, and I knew he'd be interested. That might have been what stopped me—every time our conversation lulled and I thought about bringing it up, it would strike me how totally interested in it he'd be, and the words would stop just shy of my mouth. The legend of the bear, of course, was its invincibility, and Paul Diver struck me as the sort of person who wanted himself to be invincible and therefore maybe to take that away from anyone else.

But the second time I saw the bear, we were together. Paul Diver saw him too. He nearly fell over, he was so excited.

"It's a bear," he said impulsively, gripping me so tightly his overgrown nails dug into my shoulders. "A *bear!*"

"I see it."

We were crouched behind a log out of fear and instinct, up toward the top of a ridge. The bear was down in the valley below, not looking at us, just picking its way through some underbrush. It was smaller than I would've expected, although maybe this was just from the distance. Its fur was as dark as my own hair and kind of a similar color, like stained wood. Nudging its nose around in the grass, twitching its little ears every so often. It was unnerving seeing a wild bear, life-sized and in daylight. It was sort of lumpy looking.

"I've never seen a bear around here before, *never*," said Paul Diver.

"Me neither."

"You've only been here a few weeks, though, that's nothing. I've been here *forever*." He leaned forward on the log, stretching himself up a bit. "You think it's that one bear?"

"What one bear?" I asked, already knowing.

"The one loose from the Smokies, back in June or something."

I squinted. I'd known for a while now that I needed glasses, but I still didn't have any. All the same, I could tell it was a pretty normal-looking bear, but not for around here.

I was about to tell him this wasn't the same bear, but as soon as I opened my mouth, the bear swiveled its head around and stared at me.

"Holy shit!" Paul Diver shivered and grabbed my arm. "It's looking right at me!"

It wasn't, I knew. The bear was looking at me and me only.

"Maybe it'll charge us," I said. "Should we move?"

"You chicken?" he whispered instantly.

"Why do you keep doing that? I don't think it really works on me."

He ignored me. "Okay," he said, after a moment. "Okay, yeah, we should move."

***

That night, my uncle asked me where I was off to all the time. "Not that I mind you exploring and all," he said. "It's healthy. Just want to make sure you're safe."

We were sitting in his living room, him on his armchair and me on the couch, eating a meat lovers' pizza he'd brought back from town. "I made a friend," I said. "A kid who lives back in the hills."

"What hills?"

I still wasn't sure exactly, so I pointed in the general direction I'd walk in to find Paul Diver, deeper into the valley.

My uncle frowned, bristling his mustache. "Nobody else lives around here," he said. "Nobody with kids, anyway."

"His dad works for the park, like you. Elmer Diver?"

"I don't know any Elmer Diver," said my uncle. He took a big bite of pizza, chewed thoughtfully, and swallowed. "I guess maybe I don't know everybody, though. You ever met this kid's dad? Been to his house?"

"No." I was starting to feel a tinge of queasiness, although I couldn't have said why. After all, it wasn't as though me and this boy were breaking any rules.

"Hmm." My uncle swallowed another bite of pizza, nodded again. "Well, the next time you see him, bring him 'round, okay? I'd be happy to make him dinner." Belatedly he seemed to notice the half-eaten slice of pizza he was holding and smiled abashedly. "I mean really make it."

"Okay," I said.

"How often do you see him?"

"Not very often," I lied.

The summer went on and I didn't invite Paul Diver over to my house, just like he didn't invite me to his. But we kept seeing each other, practically every day. I stopped getting letters from Allen after a while, but I didn't mind. We hadn't had much to talk about anyway without a game between us, and Paul Diver and I had real things to spend our time on, man things. We found a small pond at the base of a waterfall and passed a lot of afternoons swimming in it, and he taught me how to shoot one of his father's rifles.

"Is this legal?" I asked him once.

"God, *is this legal.* Do you hear yourself sometimes?"

We kept seeing the bear, too, gradually more often and from shorter and shorter distances. August was when things got really bad. My uncle told me he was probably going to send me home in a couple of weeks so I could catch the start of the school year, and suddenly it was like that bear was everywhere. I'd hear it rustling in the bushes when I stepped off the path to pee; I'd see it lumbering off the side of the road and realize at the last second it was really a deer. It showed up in my dreams most nights, and I'd hear bumps against my window and jolt upright in bed, sweating, not knowing whether the sound had been real. Once or twice, I peered out through the curtains and thought I saw a dark shape rumbling back into the shadows. I could feel the dread all the way to my bones, every day: a vague foreboding, with a reason I couldn't or didn't want to name.

I didn't tell my uncle and I didn't tell Paul Diver, either, but he learned anyway. "You need to get more sleep!" he told me once, laughing. "Your eyeballs look like big black holes."

One day the bear loped past us in the woods: a rustling of branches and leaves, a thundering, a streak of brown close enough I could almost feel the air brush my neck as it passed. Then it was gone. Paul Diver said something, but I didn't hear; I stumbled a couple of steps and vomited against the base of a tree.

"Jeez," he said, putting his hand on my back. "That bear's got you really worked up, huh?"

"I guess." I wasn't sure it really was the bear, but this I absolutely couldn't say. The other looming thing, the one of my going home pretty soon, was something I couldn't speak of aloud.

"Well," said Paul Diver, after a moment. He straightened up and brushed the dirt off his pants. "I know what we have to do."

"What's that?"

"You're going to have to touch that bear."

My body went stiff. "What?"

"You heard me. Only way to get rid of all that fear is to take charge," he said. He put his hands on his hips and grinned at me, and in that grin I thought I saw something darker—something that had maybe been there the whole time—but I didn't look away.

He must have sensed my hesitation because his face softened a little. "Just one touch," he said quietly. "That's all. And the bear wouldn't get hurt and neither would you."

I had no idea how touching a bear would work in practice. But I was looking into Paul Diver's eyes and he seemed to know, and it did seem tempting, after letting the idea sit between my ears for a moment—to know that I'd touched a bear and lived, to not have to be afraid of anything anymore.

A stranger approaches you in the forest. He can touch a bear without dying and knows how to help you. What do you do?

"Okay," I said. I felt like there was another question I ought to be asking, but I didn't know what it was, so I ignored it. "Okay, let's do it."

***

I thought it would be a while before the bear showed up again, but it wasn't. There was no time to think about it, no time to weigh my options or change my mind. The very next day, we were swimming at one of our usual waterfalls when Paul Diver splashed out of the water, pointing frantically with one pale, slick arm. "Look! There he is! I see him!"

A shot of reluctance coursed through me, but I tried forcing it down because, after all, I'd said I would do this. And didn't I want to touch the bear? I turned around and there it was, several yards away, half-turned away from us and sniffing at the base of a tree. Its hide shifted with every movement, shining bright brown under a patch of late sun. There was no slant in the ground or anything; the animal was level with us, and probably looked further away than it was. It didn't even turn its head at the sound of the splashing; it didn't notice, or maybe didn't care.

Paul Diver scrambled up out of the water, and without thinking, I followed him. We'd been practicing shooting earlier, and he'd left his father's rifle on the ground by our clothes. He picked it up, offered it to me.

"What?" I said. "I thought—"

"We're not gonna kill it, silly," said Paul Diver. "Not if you don't want to. But we *are* gonna have to shoot it if you want to get close enough to touch it."

When I didn't respond, he pressed the rifle into my hand, his eyes glittering.

"Think about it," he said, in the same light voice as always. "That bear can withstand *anything*. It got hit by a car, remember? And there's been state troopers after it all summer. It's *definitely* been shot before. One little bullet's not gonna do anything! It'll just keep the thing still long enough for you to do what you need to do. Then we all go our separate ways. Easy as that."

"We all...?"

"I mean us and the bear."

I had taken the rifle, just by not resisting him when he handed it to me. I turned back to look at where the bear had been, half-hoping it would be gone again, but it wasn't. The dumb thing wasn't even looking at me.

Slowly, Paul Diver moved my arms so I was lifting the gun, maneuvered so it was pointing at the bear.

But what if it wasn't the same bear? What if all summer, people had just been attacking innocent bears, all making it into something it wasn't, just for the sake of having something to hunt down?

1. *Shoot the bear.*
2. *Shoot the bear.*
3. *Shoot the bear.*
4. *Shoot the bear.*

Was this what I'd come to the Black Hills to do? I wondered. Becoming a man, was this it? Would I feel it when it happened? Would the bear, like the gray jay, come back to me night after night, would it someday do to me what I'd done to it? Would my uncle be proud—confused—disgusted? Then I was thinking about my father and what he might think or do when the gun went off, my finger over its trigger, and then the bear went down.

My breath staggered in my throat, and I stumbled back from the kick of the gun. It was nothing like killing a bear in a game. Paul Diver whooped and hollered and clapped me on the back. I dropped the gun, but he must have been expecting that because he caught it before it hit the ground, saying, "Easy there, tiger."

Then he skipped up through the trees, toward the bear lying on its side. I had no choice but to follow. I heard every one of my footsteps, every twig, every leaf. Every shifting in the trees.

When I reached the bear, it was breathing shallowly, lying in an awkward position with one of its forelegs under its body and staring into the ground with glassy eyes.

"Go on!" Paul Diver told me. "Your closure awaits!"

"You lied," I said, still looking at the bear. My voice was trembling. I'd left my shirt back by the water, and although it was summer, the skin of my torso felt suddenly bare and cold without it.

"What? C'mon, no I didn't."

"You said it would be fine. It's not fine, it's dying."

"C'mon, man." He giggled. "You know you're not that stupid."

I was speechless. At my knees, the bear lay still.

"Or maybe you are, I dunno. Either way, don't make this all be for nothing! Go on, touch him! He won't bite!" He laughed as if he'd just told a funny joke, and then reached down himself and slapped the bloody fur of the bear, hard, to prove he could.

My reaction was instant, searing revulsion. The cool dread I'd felt back when I'd first seen him skinning the bird suddenly slid into place with sharp clarity. "Go away," I said.

He looked at me, surprised. "What? What did I do?"

"Go away go away go the *fuck away*!"

"Hey," he said, the surprise on his face turning to anger. "I'm trying to help you here."

"FUCK OUT OF MY LIFE!" I screamed, stepping forward and shoving him. I couldn't believe I'd done this—just for the sake of feeling better, I'd done something like this. My lower lip began to tremble.

Paul Diver stumbled back a couple of paces and shook his head at me disdainfully. For a moment I thought he was going to say something really awful, but he didn't; the look said it all. Then he turned and walked off through the trees, on no path at all, the rifle hanging low at his side.

I sat down next to the bear and tried to think about what the right thing to do would be. When you've just killed a bear, do you comfort it? Do you touch it after all? Do you go and tell your uncle, who at this point is sending you home anyway and might be able to help?

I decided to sit down next to the bear and die with it out of respect. I had no way of making myself die, but my thoughts weren't making a whole lot of sense at the time and I just sort of assumed it would happen naturally.

I didn't die, of course. A couple of times I tried closing my eyes and imagining I had. But at the end of the day, the bear was the only one who died. The sun set early that evening and I went home.

***

Later that night, I sat outside on my uncle's porch, watching the dark trees and not saying anything. The white electric fan was still standing by the door, humming around in slow circles. I'd decided not to tell my uncle, or anybody at all, about the bear. He came and sat down next to me after a while and offered me a soda, but I didn't take it.

"You were out late today," he said.

"Sorry."

"You ever see that kid again? That kid you were friends with?"

I shook my head. "I think we grew apart," I said.

He nodded. He was looking out at the trees, too, but my uncle sometimes had a way of making it feel like he was looking at you, even when he was facing a different direction. "You know," he said, "I know you're not looking forward to going home. I wouldn't be either, if I were you. I wish there was more I could do about it." He reached over and ruffled my hair. "But you're going to be okay, you know? You're a smart kid. And a good kid, which is what's most important. You'll be okay. You've got a good heart." He paused, then stood up abruptly, as though realizing too late he'd become sentimental, and went back inside.

I reached up to my neck and fingered the bear tooth I'd tied there using a string, and stuck it into my thumb hard enough to feel a pinprick of blood appear. I thought about how long a future was waiting for me back at home, and I dug the tooth in deeper past my skin and knew the wet ruby pearls that were growing and spreading there, not seen but felt.

Indicative of Something Much Worse

Harriett Sanford is never getting her hand back. She knows it, of course—why else would she go to all this trouble, striding out into the dark woods the first night of summer session, coming back and washing the blood off in the river, cursing Emily Meredith and then each of our cabins one by one? She'll never forgive us. It's gone and she will never, ever forgive us.

***

I begged my parents for as many weeks at camp as they could possibly manage, and they said they could manage one. I came prepared. I brought three changes of clothes, bug spray, pads in a plastic bag squished far in the bottom of my trunk, lots of Oreos, a headlamp I bought at Target with my best friend Lily, and a big old giant crush on Cody Alves.

Cody Alves is so sweet, so dorky. So good. He's not the most athletic boy counselor, nor even the most crushed-upon. He's awkward; the only things he's really good at are water polo and making kids smile. And arts and crafts—he's the Arts and Crafts Leader this summer and can carve himself a chessboard like nobody's business. He never complains. Camp is hot and mosquito-ridden, and while we eat good food three or four times a day, everyone's always hungry, homesick, injured in some minor way, left out of a fun game, or scared of the dark—and while we love this suffering, in fact look forward to it year-round, we also complain about it wholeheartedly. Cody never does, and that's what makes him magic, what makes him a grownup. What makes kids like me love him.

He's there when my parents pull up the gravel drive with me and Lily carpooling in the backseat—waving from the fence along with the other senior counselors: Tyler Halloway, Dinah Randall, Emily Meredith. My mom does a little tight-lipped scowl when she sees Emily Meredith.

When she signed me up this year, she wanted to call the camp director—Jimmy this year, a junior in college—to ask for me not to be placed in the same cabin as Emily. I had to beg her not to—if Jimmy knew, *everyone* would know, and I was a counselor-in-training this year—nobody would take me seriously if they knew my *mom* was making *phone calls*—and besides, I thought frantically but did not add aloud to my argument: Emily would hate me.

Cars huddle in the gravel under a glaring Indiana July sun. The counselors pair up to haul the arriving campers' trunks to the cabins—as CITs, Lily and I have to help this year, and it only takes two trips lugging trunks up the knotty hills before my arm muscles start burning. We hug my parents goodbye and watch them recede down the drive, under the leafy crowns of the red maple and beech trees. The air stirs; mosquitos have already gotten to my ankles.

And they're gone, just like that. By seven in the evening, Jimmy at twenty-three is the oldest person left here. As always, I feel a jerk of sadness when the bumper of my parents' car vanishes into the green leaves—a twinge of sleepover-homesickness, like I just grew all the way up, here and now, and wait, did I really want to do that—but then there are hot dogs to roast, and cabinmates to meet, and Lily is tugging me toward the Big Field for capture the flag.

Only when my parents are gone do I catch my first glimpse of Harriett. She's one year younger than me and has stringy, ghost-white hair. She's standing on the porch of the front cabin, eating a candy bar and looking around at everyone while Jimmy wrangles counselors with his clipboard. My stomach plummets when I see her, and I'm not even sure why.

Lily catches me staring and nudges me. "Come explore with me?" she asks, but I can tell from her voice there's something else she wants urgently to say.

We're barely to the mess cabin when she stops and looks over at me darkly.

She asks, "Have you been dreaming about her too?"

***

It happened over winter session. Only real camp loyalists go to winter session: a co-ed week in the woods during the coldest weather, with polar plunges, garbage-lid sledding, snowshoe-making in the arts and crafts cabin, and cozy nights clutching hot cocoa mugs in gloved hands. Instead of the shelters, which have roofs but are largely open to the elements and deer and spiders, winter campers sleep in piles of blankets and quilts in the mess cabin, which is unheated but has sealed walls and a door that shuts and locks.

The kids who go to winter session are kids like Harriett, whose parents send them to camp all summer long: six weeks, eight weeks. Very wealthy, in other words, and fine being away from their kids for months on end. Some years, the winter session kids build snow forts and have wars; some years they don't even get snow and spend the whole time playing board games and frigid rounds of tag in the frost, baking instant brownies in stovetop pots.

Last year was a no-snow year. We all heard the truth from Dayton, who was there and who came home with the least hesitation to spread the story around. The counselors had to get creative coming up with activities. On the third day, when everyone was sick to death of Monopoly and scary stories, Emily Meredith had an idea: they could play Survivor.

Who can stand outside the longest without their shirt on?

Which team can beat the other to the end of the obstacle course?

Who can name the most presidents?

Who can hold their hand the longest in the river?

***

Coming back to summer camp ready to enact a vengeful curse is one thing, but Harriett isn't even shy about it. She hits the ground running. Everyone is giving her odd looks from the first night, and although it could be because we all know what happened winter session—we remember the uproar, the hospital stay, the time she was out of school, the *lawsuit*—it's not really about that. It's because all the counselors have been dreaming about her.

"How could she even do that, though?"

Tyler—Emily Meredith's boyfriend, a basketball player during the school year—is trying to make us see reason in the commissary shelter. There are only a few counselors constellated around; I wasn't invited into this conversation, but I've edged my way in, by way of standing near Lily. Lily always knows how to become involved in things without really Involving Herself. The ends of my ponytail are sticking to the back of my neck and my tee shirt, and I'm trying not to think about my bug bites.

Tyler's got his arm wrapped loose around Emily. He grins, then tries to look very serious. "I'm just thinking, probably," he says, "I mean, most likely—" He removes his arm and knots his fingers together contemplatively in his lap. "I think we all just feel really bad about what happened," he says in a low voice, looking around the scattering of teenagers, making eye contact. He even makes eye contact with me, which makes me shudder—automatically, because it's Tyler Halloway Eye Contact, and although I don't have a crush on him personally, shuddering is just what I've heard you do—and then I have to actively remind myself: He's not talking about *me*, right? I wasn't there. Doesn't he know I wasn't there?

"So," Tyler says, "if we're having—I mean, if some of us have had—" He waves his hand, a loose flop of the wrist in lieu of the word *dreams*. "It's a psychological thing," he says. "I think it makes perfect sense."

The senior counselors who were there at winter session: Tyler. Max Shoku and Ava Serratelli, who both resigned and haven't been back since. Dinah Randall. Emily Meredith.

Jimmy wasn't there, and he isn't here now. The camp director's job is a busy one, and it's best not to bother them with random stresses; last year's director, Andrew, yelled at a CIT until she cried for not using hydrogen peroxide when she bandaged a camper's skinned knee. Lily and I overheard them while walking down one of the trails to the lake. She said she couldn't remember what she was supposed to do. How did she not know, he demanded, three weeks into camp? And why was her response to just guess and hope she got away with it? Why would she not ask for help? The fact that she would respond this way wasn't only a safety issue; it was indicative of something much worse, indicative of something about her as a person.

Dinah glances at Tyler and Emily, then over to me and Lily. When her gaze lands on us, it's like she's not sure why we're even there.

"Well, what did she—do?" she asks. "In everyone else's dreams?"

Lily's not smiling, but I can tell she appreciates the intrigue of this.

It's Emily who speaks first.

"It was like our hands changed," she said. "Her hands were mine, and mine were hers. We were making friendship bracelets with each other's hands." She's been looking down at her hands while saying this, and now she looks up—but not at anyone, just into the empty air out past the shelter, out into the dark, open woods. Her shoulders hang forward. "It wasn't even really that scary," she says, but then as she's saying it, she starts crying.

***

On the second day, Lily says she wants to sneak out later and go night swimming.

Camp is made for things like this. All the counselors are in high school or early college, and while there are waivers and phones in the front cabin and protocols in place, it's still meant to be a place known for its freedoms. A place where you can just *be a kid*, which tradition has decided usually means doing insane things your parents would never let you do, and then never—on pain of being uncool, of being frozen out of every social situation for the rest of your childhood—telling anyone.

When I nudge her that night, Lily blinks awake and then mumbles, no, she's actually so tired. I'm tired too. We've been building the towering skeletons of bonfires, chasing little kids around all day.

And I'm not very surprised: Lily's my best friend, but she has no follow through. She darts from urge to urge, smiles often and warmly but cannot be counted on. I never believe anything she says, except that she loves me.

It's a few hours later—I have no idea what time; we can't have our phones at camp—when the low sounds of giggling voices tug me again from sleep. I think I imagined them, and I'm just drifting off when I hear them again. They surface every few seconds, moving in low rises and dips, like bubbles from water. I can't make out what they're saying.

I slide into my flip-flops and move from the shelter, clutching my headlight, but I never turn it on; I just step slowly down the winding trails, padding over rocks and roots and through the warm night where the dew is brewing, until I reach the slope of trees leading down to the lake.

Even through the fluttering branches of shadow folded over the water, I can see them: Emily and Dinah, in to their necks, splashing around. Lily is with them, wearing a confidential, nervous grin that matches theirs. The *s*'s and *sh*'s in their whispers slice around in the night air. It seems impossible that I could've heard them from so far away, from all across camp, slipping into my half-dreams like mermaids, like fairies. The crescent moon sits on the water in the middle of their circle like a plated offering, but they keep breaking it up.

***

The next day, I steer clear of Lily, of all of them. I couldn't put words to why I feel I've been wronged—maybe it was an impromptu gathering, maybe there was some plausible reason I couldn't be invited—and if I tried to say it out loud to Lily, I already know I'd sound like a kid left out of a fun game at recess. I try to be mature.

The CITs are in charge of gathering wood and building the daily bonfire. I carve a path out on the other side of the lake, where no one else would go. I bend fallen limbs up toward me and stomp on them where they're weak, splinter them into things I can carry.

By eleven or so, sweat is pouring off my forehead, sticking in my brows. Once, as a kid, I got lost out here and Emily Meredith—three years older than me, the sorority-bound angel I have always secretly wanted to be—found me a few hours later, crying. She laughed like it was no problem at all. She made me feel like I hadn't been stupid to be scared—and what's more, like I wasn't even a kid, like I was someone old enough and cool and fun enough to even be her friend.

"Everyone gets lost out here," she told me. "Once, we were having this all-camp water balloon war, and I ran so far into the woods, they had to come out with *flashlights*. I was so embarrassed." And she led me back to camp just in time for dinner, and then she vanished into the summer evening to stand around the limp tetherballs talking and smiling with the older girls, her friends. But I've always felt like in her kindness she let me in on a secret. Now, as a counselor, it's my sacred duty to keep it, and only pass it on to kids I can trust.

The secret is something like, *It's okay.* Something like, *Everyone makes mistakes.*

Arms full of dead limbs, I trudge back around the lip of the lake. I'm almost past the reedy eastern edge when I hear something almost too light to be a splash—more like a tap-tap. I turn and look, and a moment later a wet crown of white hair rises through the water.

I start, and the dry birch and sassafras limbs tumble to the ground. It's Harriett Sanford: she pushes her hair back out of her face with her one hand and squints at me. She's standing where the water bugs skip around, where sometimes we dig in the mud for crawdads. I've camped on the lakeshore before and seen the pale morning sun flatten out like an egg cracked too soon, right where she's standing.

"Harriett—you scared me."

"You didn't see me?"

"No," I say, letting myself sound a little angry. But then I force out a laugh, because technically I'm a counselor-in-training, and she's still a camper, which means I'm required to be the bigger person.

"You weren't invited last night, were you?" she asks. She drops back down again a bit, letting the lake water close over her shoulders, so she's just a head. "When they all went out?"

I frown at her. "How'd you know they went out?"

"How'd you *not* know?"

I feel a little pang of hurt at this. The little derisive smile she's giving me—it's too familiar. "I was asleep."

"I know," she says lazily. She dips her head back to feel the cold, to look up at the sunny sky.

I bend and start gathering the wood up again. I might not know *everything* that goes on, I think—like I might not know when important conversations are happening, or when Lily's out doing fun things without me—but I know Harriett is running around casting revenge spells, doing witchy vengeance rituals. I'm at least not too out of it to know that. On Tuesday, the lake turned red for a few hours and we had to cancel swim time; I didn't see the red water myself, but I was there when Cody and Tyler were whispering about it at the craft shack. Yesterday Dinah Randall woke up with spiders in her hair, then didn't speak all day, ashen-faced, and then just after sunset cut all her hair off.

"Harriett," I say—and then, suddenly, counselor-urge kicks in. All I'm feeling is frustration and confusion, but magically I soften my voice. I try to figure out a way to be kind. Like someone you can confide in—someone who gets it. "Harriett, can I—like, help you somehow? I mean, where's this all coming from?"

She tilts her head back up. "*You* weren't even there," she says. "You don't have to know."

"But I want to."

She looks right at me. I forget for a second that she isn't a myth, that she's a kid just like me. Months ago, sitting and phone-scrolling on Lily's bedroom floor, my best friend looked up and asked in an urgent whisper—*dude, did you know Harriett's going back to camp? I mean, isn't that fucked up?*

"I love it here," she says. "I love it and they don't deserve to take it away, not even by accident."

"But—I mean, it *was* an accident," I say weakly. "Emily—I mean, none of them really *knew*, like..."

"It's not my fucking fault," she says, "that they're idiots."

We're not allowed to cuss at camp, is the first thing I think. For the first time I see a little of her own anger in her eyes, in her jaw—the anger that's fueling her, that crept into and soured everyone's dreams. "It's not even the hand thing, really," she says, a new sharpness creeping into her voice. "It's that I lost *anything*. Because I wanted them to like me."

***

Emily's tooth disappears in the middle of the night. She wakes up and feels a hole with her tongue: a liquid thickness in her mouth, which becomes a stinging cave when she pokes it. Her campers wake to the sound of her crying. Headlight beams flick on, and there she is: mouth stupidly open, hazard-red forming a line down her chin. Tender, and gaping, and gummy-red: it feels just the way it did when she was a little kid.

The next day, Harriett Sanford comes to breakfast with a squarish molar looped around her neck on a string.

She says she found it in the river.

***

Dayton saw it all happen. He spread the word at his friends' houses, in the hallways at school.

Harriett and Tyler were the only ones left with their hands plunged into the icy river. But Tyler was a senior in high school, and his hand was twice the size of Harriett's. He kept grinning at her in a way that said, *We all already know I'm better than you; why not confirm it? Go ahead, go ahead, quit. No one has been thinking about you this whole time; right now is the only time any of us are even looking at you. You are short and awkward and not pretty. Give up, give up, go back to your cabin and stop fucking existing.*

Okay, this part I imagine. All Dayton mentioned was a grin—but I know the kind he meant.

And Emily, Tyler's girlfriend, was grinning too, encouraging her. *Come ON, Harriett, you can beat this smug jerk. Show him who's the boss. YOU'RE the boss, am I right? God, Harriett, I never knew you were so hardcore! Look, she's STILL GOING! Ha-rri-ett. Ha-rri-ett, Ha-rri-ett, nonono, don't give up NOW, do NOT give him the satisfaction—*

The three or four other campers cheered and chanted along with her—until they noticed how gray Harriett was turning, how weak she looked, how her eyes were tearing up. But Emily kept going—she wanted to keep the energy up, wanted everyone to have fun, didn't seem to notice.

Tyler was peeved when he finally yanked his reddened hand out, shaking the icy droplets off—"Okay, *damn* then, she wins, get the kid her brownies"—and Harriett exhaled a scraggly sigh of relief as she withdrew her hand from the water. She kept looking at her hand, though, and breathing roughly.

Within a few minutes, she started to scream.

***

Dayton said no one knew what to do, everyone was panicking. Inside, they got Harriett wrapped all in blankets; they tried running her blistering fingers under the tap, and it only made her scream worse. They made a fire in the fireplace and had her sit in front of it with gloves on, and all the other campers huddled far away from her, moving around restlessly while she stared into the flames, eyebrows arched furiously, eyes burning. She didn't close her mouth all evening: even silent, she was gaping, she was rigid. She seemed not to notice anymore she was crying.

The mess cabin was frosty, even with the doors closed and spare blankets stuffed in their creases—but Emily Meredith was in a terror of her own now, pacing around, muttering with Tyler and Dinah in words the campers couldn't hear. They made everyone go to sleep, Harriett still sniffling. They said she was just upset—which made perfect sense; did she need anything, more hot chocolate? She should have some more hot chocolate—and after some good sleep in front of the fire, she'd feel so much better in the morning.

So it was over twelve hours, in the end, before they called someone. By six in the morning, another dam had broken and

Harriett was crying again, and the glove had peeled blood from her hand, her fingers had gone from white to dark blue.

"It wasn't that bad yesterday, right?" Emily asked after she hung up and the ambulance was on its way. Her own eyes were shiny, but beneath the prickling tears, more than anything, she looked focused. She focused on her boyfriend. "Like, yesterday. We all saw it. And it didn't look that bad, right? Plus, *she* was keeping it in the water, she could've just took her hand out, right? Like, we couldn't have known. I think this is the best thing we could've done."

This was the story Lily and I heard—the one our parents heard, when all the senior counselors from winter session were allowed to come back to camp, after many more first aid trainings and talks amongst themselves. It didn't look as bad as it wound up being; Harriett said she was okay, probably, initially; they did the best they could. By the time the ambulance got Harriett to the hospital, everyone was saying the same words.

***

Yet we all came back to camp. We picked out our best shirts and snacks and brought our journals. When we learned Harriett was returning too, we were a little murkily disappointed, although we'd all liked her fine enough in previous years. There was something we didn't want to be reminded of, and we were when she looked in our eyes.

***

I wake with strange lumps underneath my pillow. I roll over, half-awake, and a knuckle crunches. I sit up cold, a buzz opening my throat. I already know. I reach beneath my pillow. I pull out Harriett Sanford's crumpled hand.

I gasp and scramble from bed, but when I turn over my sheets again, I can't find it. A couple of my campers stare at me through sleepy eyes, like raccoons.

I wish I had it, because the next time I see Harriett I want to throw it at her. I want to scream at her. And the thing I want to scream most isn't *how could you*, or *what's your problem*—it's, *Harriett, who taught you all of this?*—no one taught *me* all of this.

I can't believe I'm jealous of this, too.

***

She finds me building the bonfire again on Friday, no other CITs in sight. It's the hardest job and none of them are helping me do it. Lily apologized when she last saw me an hour ago, said Dinah needed some help leading the cats-in-the-cradle activity and she'd be back as soon as she could.

Why didn't Dinah ask *me*? My limbs are aching, I am un-thought-of by everyone in the woods except maybe the woods themselves. And I'm fourteen, and it's not enough.

I know for a fact they are not thinking of me as they giggle and loop their pastel strings through cradles with the younger kids, as I prick my thumbs on green briar and construct a fire taller than me, which we'll all get credit for—unless it doesn't light, and then I alone will get blamed. Sweat slips off my neck, into the collar of my T-shirt I picked out so carefully.

My neck is bent over the tinder at the fire's heart, the amassment of twigs so tiny and thin, it's hard to imagine they could ever be useful. But this is the part we always spend the longest on; these tiny things make or break whether it burns at all. I crouch and work on the teepee until an ache sprouts across my neck, and when I finally look up, I'm not sure how long Harriett Sanford has been standing there.

She's drinking a juice box, and my first thought is *somehow I'm going to be responsible for throwing that away*. At her feet is a stuffed daypack. She looks all innocent, like she doesn't know she's caught me at the perfect moment.

Maybe, it occurs to me dully, growing up isn't learning anything. It's just swapping one secret for another—and maybe this is the one I want. The one that will look at me.

"Want some help?" she asks.

It's nice of her to offer, I think. For a moment I wonder if Harriett could just be that—a nice person. I wonder if it would matter to me either way.

***

Later, I'm crossing the Big Field when Lily catches my eye. She jerks her head, just once, and then she's walking straight again, making her way up the opposite slope and toward the riflery range. It's such a quick look, I might've missed it, but I understand. You have to be quick, to get by at camp.

I catch her before the bridge, and by the time we reach the range, we're walking with two other counselors. "Clear the range," calls Lily, and the resounding *clear* comes back seconds later, but I can't tell whose voice it is.

There wasn't a scheduled staff meeting, but still almost everyone is here. Cody is sitting on top of the lockbox, crocheting a scraggly scarf he must've brought from the arts and crafts cabin. Lily sits on the log railing next to Dinah, and they start kicking their legs in time, dangling their toes inches above the splintering wood floor. Tyler is sitting next to Emily on the far side of the floor, but he looks uncomfortable, isn't meeting anyone's eyes. Jimmy is here, and he looks like he wants to die.

"All right," says Jimmy. "So—I've noticed some of us—some of you—have been feeling a little unsettled, lately, with various stuff going on." He holds his clipboard loosely in one hand. He looks very camp-fashionable: a grizzly beard growing, wonky glasses, an old yellow bandana tied around his neck.

"I feel like it's obvious," said Emily hoarsely. "I feel like we need to call her parents."

The air prickles up. A voice snakes through my head, but I don't even know if it's mine. It's like hearing the shadows of the woods passing through me. *Oh, now,* they say, *now, you want to call her parents?*

Lily and Dinah both give an involuntary shiver.

"Well—hang on," says Jimmy. He tries to pretend he's giving this due, objective thought. But he's the camp director: he knows parents should've been called well before now. "I think," he says, trying to find the right phrase, "well—the kids seem to be doing okay, right? It seems to be, like, it's just *us*—" He laughs. "It's just us counselors really being *bothered* by things." By *bothered by things*, one can only assume he means *afflicted by witchcraft*. "So, maybe—if the kids are all having a good time, doing okay—and safe—then I think we're doing our jobs! I mean, that's what we're all here for. The important thing always is that the kids are having fun," he says seriously, like we've neglected our jobs by forgetting this.

As a kid growing up here, I was constantly having fun. All year at school, pretty much nothing happens. We grow up on seven or fourteen or twenty-one nights a year: the slim weeks we spend at camp, when everything explodes. Those days were so vivid when I was eight, when I was ten. I cataloged every time Cody smiled at me, every time Emily talked to me.

And after all that, I actually don't feel all golden now, to be included. I look around and think, it's official: I've been scammed. I was invited to the lame party cleanup but not the actual party. When did they have it without me?

Did it even fucking happen? Or is this all I've been looking in on?

Looking around, I catch Cody's eye by accident and he smiles geekishly. *Oh*, I think, my heart crumpling softly apart. I feel warm here, sun-dappled in the nest of woods—the riflery range is tiny and far away from the Big Field, secluded and not often actually used for riflery, so it's always where secret meetings are held. It's not two hours ago that I finished building the fire with Harriett, and now I'm at the secret meeting with all these people who when school starts I will feel like such a celebrity if they invite me to their lockers, and I almost warn them. But I don't.

***

Afterward, I stalk toward the mess cabin with Lily at my side.

"You didn't help me build the fire today."

"What?"

I don't want to repeat myself, but thankfully she recovers before I have to.

"No," she says, a little dumbfounded. "I was helping Dinah. I told you that."

"Yeah, but you could've come after."

"No, I couldn't. It took the whole time."

I don't believe her. I'm walking angrily fast, but she's keeping up with me. I stub my toe on a root hidden in the grass and pitch forward, and her arm shoots out, but I catch myself. My toe throbs.

"No one else on staff helped, either."

"Well, I'm *sorry*," she says, a little irritated.

I don't even want her to be sorry. I only want her to know what it is I'm mad about. "It's just really hard work." I shake my head, slowing my pace. We're getting close to the mess cabin, entering the realm of other people's hearing. "Harriett helped me. She offered."

I can tell Lily's confused by this. Normally we should be whispering suspicions of Harriett; Lily doesn't quite know what to say when her name is brought up just like this, flatly, with no blame or joke riding along with the words. Like she's just a regular fellow person, named Harriett, and we can call her that in our normal voices.

I know what Lily's going to do, and I'm tired even before she does it. I want to tell her, *just stop, please, stop.*

But she does it: her eyes go light, and she tries making a joke, her voice low and conspiratorial. "Did she do anything witchy to the fire?"

But I don't laugh, or even smile, and it's not a joke anyway.

When I say nothing, her gaze on me turns more careful. Then she looks away, to the ultimate frisbee game happening over on the lawn; everything smells like cut grass and horse manure. Mosquitos snip at the air. "Oh my god. You're acting like *I'm* the one being mean."

"It's not about *you*. I just kind of think—I mean, it probably did feel pretty shitty." I'm thinking about Harriett's hand freezing up, all her nerve endings detaching themselves while Emily Meredith watched, smiling, not bothering to know about it. I want Lily to understand, but I can't find the right words. "Like, having that happen, like, in front of everybody?"

"I mean, yeah. Obviously, I feel for her," says Lily impatiently. "I feel really bad about it. We all do. What do you want us to do? Give her some hugs? Write her an apology card?"

She's annoyed at me, and suddenly I know, looking at her, she's going to share that annoyance later. The way they all look at Harriett—the way they look at each other when they *talk* about Harriett—it's the same way they all have looked for years, it's the whole reason she put her hand in. And Lily's going to do that to me. I'm her best friend, but she's still going to go to Dinah and Emily later and tell them all what I've said, how weird I'm being. *Has Harriett gotten to her, cursed her?* And Lily could just talk straight to me. But she won't. The spite she feels for me, she's going to unload it in other rooms.

"Don't do it, Lily," I say, my voice cracking. I didn't even realize I felt sad until now.

Her eyes have gone huge. "Do *what*?"

"I don't know—I don't know."

"God, sometimes—" She rolls her eyes. "Never mind. I'm hungry. I'll see you later."

***

At campfire our legs kick under us. It's like we're swimming. We don't even notice the grassy ground, except as another thing propelling our bare feet forward. We dance, run and pinwheel around it, working out the last crazed flare of energy from the day while counselors play on their guitars all loud and magnetic.

When we all settle into the grass, kids start picking their way up, taking turns singing softer songs, telling stories and jokes with way-too-long setups. The stars facing us get bored and start walking away. Lily goes up with her guitar, and she and Dinah sing a beautiful folk song with a harmony I can tell they must've practiced for at least an hour. They close their eyes, threading the melody together like a soft seam of water unfolding at your toe's touch, invisible under the lake—and when the song finishes, they open their eyes and smile the same smile.

The fire was built six or seven feet tall; it's down to three or four now. And as Lily and Dinah move to take their seats, the first couple of gasps bite into the night.

I glance around. Lily and Dinah haven't quite sat down yet; they look woozy now, frowning. Lily blinks slowly down at her hands.

Someone nearby has been breathing heavily, and I haven't been noticing. I look over now to see Cody Alves, panting, sweating profusely and pulling in long, ragged breaths. He stands up and starts staggering back a few steps.

"Do you guys feel hot?" asks Jimmy.

"Everyone back up from the fire, back up," says Emily Meredith, herding her kids back over the grass.

My palms are sweating. I'm still sitting cross-legged, too nervous even to twitch. I look at Harriett, but she's looking at the fire.

From her daypack, when we built the fire earlier today, she unloaded: one of Jimmy's clipboards with Wednesday's crumpled schedule still on it, Lily's spiral-bound journal, Tyler Halloway's navy Colts T-shirt, Dinah's beaded bracelet. A king chess piece, no bigger than a finger, that Cody Alves whittled from pine the other day; he's almost done handmaking his own complete chess set.

It's just going to make them sweat, she said, hanging the thin chain of Emily Meredith's butterfly necklace off the knot of a stacked branch. It was easy to cover these tokens in the thick fire, under layer after layer of wood. *I'm not about to traumatize a bunch of little kids, you know.*

By now, the stolen items are probably charring in the coals beneath what's left. The other counselors have all backed far off from the fire and are casting looks around, fanning themselves off, doubled over with hands on thighs. Sweating, like she said. Later tonight, thin burn scars will appear in the palm of Jimmy's hand where he clenches his clipboard, on Emily Meredith's collarbone in place of the butterfly.

For a moment I do wonder. The campers look more confused than scared, but kids always understand more than you think they do. I feel a pang of guilt, and then Cody stumbles over and grabs Harriett's shoulder.

"Come on," he says. The fire is cracking and snapping, and most of the counselors have moved to the other side of it, into the grass; I can see Lily through the flames, probably wondering why I haven't joined her.

"Come *on*," says Cody, raising his voice. "You're being cruel, Harriett."

"*You're being cruel, Harriett—*"

"Jesus *fuck*," says Cody, losing his patience. He grabs her wrist and starts pulling her away from the fire. I can't tell if he's doing it because he thinks it's right or because he just wants the situation to simmer, doesn't want any of us to get caught.

Harriett lets out a long scream like a black tunnel, with such violence, such hatred, the remaining campers shuffle back from the fire in a startled tide. She shakes Cody away and sprints right at the fire, and then someone else screams, right before she does it. In the shadow this side of the blaze she stops momentarily, tilts her head to one side and locks her eyes with mine. She is angry as all hell. Then she steps barefooted up onto the crumbling pile of logs and flame, and I learn it. The secret. Just by looking at her.

She takes in a deep red breath, eyes closed.

Then another hand sprouts from her wrist where there wasn't one before—and that's not all.

For a long time after this night, I think about this, and I think about it more as new explanations start showing up to paper over what we all saw with our own eyes. What I saw—what I still think I saw—was something that had used to be a lonely girl, twisting into something new in a blaze of firelight. No one will say so later on, but Harriett became something else that night. She showed us all how, and no one followed.

But in my dreams for weeks, months afterward, I imagine doing it. I imagine moving past Cody while a few screams send up from the grass and going to stand next to Harriett. I step onto the charcoal. Harriett doesn't open her eyes for me. Cody looks at me blankly through the bending smoke, and then it burns too much, and I can't see him anymore. Something sears beneath my feet—an initial shock—but it's not so bad, once I'm in it. Ashes crowd my ankles and I lose my footing over the coals, but then catch myself—how is it not that bad? I want to tell the others. I wish they would all come with me—with us—with her.

The adults discount what they can't imagine, but me, imagining it is all I can do. Thinking what it would have felt like—parts of myself I never even knew I had, growing in as naturally as teeth. New hands branching from my wrists and my forearms. New ears unfolding from the sides of my head, hearing more, hearing everything. Every song there is to sing at campfire, every dirty thing that has ever been said or whispered about me, everything on the planet and in my life I'm supposed to know by intuition. Wings peeling from my back, feathers and scales adding themselves to me: my back, my bare calloused feet, my heat-warmed cheeks. My flesh grows and unfurls, flower-like, it *stretches*. I realize I've been so cramped in this body, in this shelter. But it has no walls. In the dream, I can't tell anymore whether I'm being burned, somewhere beneath all this; I wonder if, all those months ago, Harriett could tell she was being burned.

The last thing I remember was the one moment of the whole thing that horrified me—the moment when she didn't look like Harriett anymore. It wasn't the flickering of animal shapes in the firelight—the sense of her becoming a bear, a deer, a falcon—it was the look in her eyes, for the last second that she had eyes. Like she hated us.

And then her whole new body was a flag of light, and the bonfire rippled high, a shower of sparks hurrying away. She left like a curtain curling upward.

We could all feel it, the moment she was gone. Goosebumps rose on my arms and I felt cold to the bone, maybe the coldest I've ever felt.

Far away from me, Lily tugged on Emily's arm and asked in a high voice, "What do we do?"

***

We all expected to be sent home, or for camp to be closed down, but it didn't happen. We didn't learn why until weeks later, a rumor fluttering around at the start of school. Jimmy called Harriett's parents late that night, after we'd coaxed the campers back into their cabins and sleeping bags—who knew what explanation he was planning to give—but her parents said she was fine. They didn't know what he was talking about. Harriett was home safe; she hadn't even gone to camp this year.

We're back at school and the leaves are turning—soon a chill will creep back into the air, and winter will come all quiet on its hind legs and cover up this year. But at night I'm stuck back in humid bedsheets, an unearthly pressure driving at my fingernails, my scapula. The fire comes back to me in fever, and I lift my feet from the coals and stamp them back down until they're numb. There are no sounds, but sometimes there's screaming. I'm about to change. The night air of the dream world curls around me, folding me into the seam where the halo of warmth from the fire opens off into cool, dark night.

I usually wake around now into the air conditioning of my bedroom, the school day waiting ahead of me and nothing left but a remnant of sweat on my brow. The kid-feeling of fear leaves me with a tremor, and everything equalizes, and I can tell I'm awake because things start feeling easier. Cold, heat, snow, fire. If you can't feel, you can't feel, but of course I could be wrong.

Paradise
after "Paradise" by John Prine

When we woke to the ash falling, we knew it was over. No phone calls were made, nobody had to guess where anyone else was. One by one, the grownups stepped outside into the pale morning, chins tilted up toward the sky, hands held out with their palms facing upward as if awaiting gifts from Jesus himself. All around them the gray ash swirled, catching sometimes in their hair and against their clothes, drifting and fluttering like snow.

    School was canceled that day because all the grownups—at least the ones who were left—were meeting up to see what to do about the Tennessee Valley Authority. None of us kids knew much about what the Tennessee Valley Authority was, but we knew it was a big company that had something to do with coal and was trying to buy everybody out. They'd bought out a lot of families already: the Buchanans, Mr. and Mrs. McNamara, the Moores and their children. None of us had been all that close with the Moore kids, which was why we hadn't thought about the company very much so far. As far as we were concerned, a company named after Tennessee could only have so much to do in Kentucky anyway, and the whole thing—the steady house-by-house takeover of land, the fumes from TVA machinery that now hung in the air—would blow over by the time the next winter rolled around.

"Maybe we shouldn't go today." Rose said it quietly, on the floor in the narrow closet next to the kitchen, while we were getting on our shoes.

I looked at her. Rose was older than me—twelve, practically a teenager—and she was plain-looking in a way that made her seem older. Brown hair parted neatly down the middle, brushed but frizzy. She was wearing a violet turtleneck and watching me with her dark eyes, in a way that seemed knowing and that I didn't entirely understand. "Why not?" I whispered because she had whispered.

"That ash. It's from the plant down the road, everyone saw it."

"We still have to go," I said, and she relented.

So we got our bikes out of the garage, met Maggie and Joseph Gilmore at their house on the way out of town, then took the dirt road out of Paradise that dead-ended at the Green River. Bike wheels whirring under us, flicking up dust. Maggie, the youngest of us at seven, had her curly pigtails flipped back over her shoulders, stray vanilla-blonde locks whipping around, coming undone as we gathered speed. The sky stewed overhead, thick and milky, but the ash fell away more and more as we got farther from town.

"Maggie," Rose said, "why are you wearing that coat?"

We biked in pairs, us boys up front and Maggie and Rose a few yards behind us, but everyone could still hear one another. Maggie's coat was thick and woolen, I had recognized it from winter, and the hood was pulled up over her head. It was May.

"So the ash won't burn my skin."

"Who told you it'd burn your skin?"

"My mom." A pause. "Didn't it burn your skin?"

"No."

"Did you feel it at all?"

"Yeah," said Rose, "but it didn't burn. I think all the heat had gone away by the time I touched it."

"Well, what did it feel like?"

Rose considered the question for a moment. "Dead skin," she said finally. "Like flakes of dead skin."

"Eww," Maggie shouted. She was younger than Rose and a girl, so she was grossed out by this sort of thing.

When we got to the river, we left our bikes in the usual place, behind some thick bushes in the grass not far from the road. Maggie shrugged off the giant coat and draped it carefully over her bike to keep it from getting in the mud. The water was stiller than usual today, moving in occasional small shudders against the banks. Golden-green like heaven, like the shimmering copper mounds at the bottom of a fountain, ridged with moss. This place was where you could get to the river most easily, but of course it went on for miles and miles, Joseph said probably four or five hundred miles at least, from our town toward the Rochester Dam and Mammoth Cave and eventually all the way up north to the Ohio. The river slipped away from Paradise here and into the deep uncertain woods where Muhlenberg County faded into forest. These were woods that we four combed afternoon after afternoon, or day after day on the weekends, and had been combing for several months now, ever since the day Michael Harris had gone missing.

Michael Harris was our hero in every sense of the word. He wore a bright red bandana, tied around his left wrist when it wasn't on his head, and he was the best of all of us at finding things to catch from the river during the summertime. Bullfrogs, every once in a while, and crawdads. None of the rest of us could find a crawdad to save our life. Joseph said he'd found one once, but he didn't show anybody and nobody had seen him catch it, and Joseph's word isn't that much good anyway. Joseph looked for river creatures the same way the rest of us did, bent down on both knees in the cold muddy grass, hands swiping around under the shallow water at the river's edge, scooping up handfuls of roly-polies and silt to drain through our fingers moments later. Not Michael Harris. Michael would jump straight in, splashing anyone who had been unlucky enough to be standing close by. He'd plunge down into the deep murky parts of the river, stay down so long we'd sometimes start to worry—Rose guessed he stayed down extra long just to scare us—and then he'd burst up again with another great splash, dark hair sopping wet and stuck to his forehead, green eyes gleaming and mouth spread wide open in a grin that dripped with river, a fat red crawdad twitching and feeling around in one fist.

    The grownups all loved Michael, too. He was nice to the teacher at school, brought her fresh Jonathan apples from the tree in his yard. He knew how to be funny in a way that grownups liked, which was different from funny in the way that kids like, although he was good at that too. If any of the rest of us had gone missing, me or Rose or Maggie or somebody, people still would have minded, but I don't think it would have torn everybody up the same way it did when Michael went.

"We should go far today," Joseph said with an air of decision as we headed down the narrow riverside path that led into the woods. We walked single file, Joseph and then me and then Rose and then Maggie, like a band of expeditioners. Joseph was wearing a tank top faded with orange stripes, and under the straps of his backpack in front of me I could see his bony shoulders, squared with determination.

"Farther than last weekend?" asked Maggie.

"A lot farther."

"How come?"

"In case we don't have much time later," said Rose.

"Well, we'll come back tomorrow," said Maggie. "And the next day."

We picked our way through the weeds and over logs, eyes still trained to the ground, since we walked down this part of the path every day and we didn't need to be looking around just yet. None of us were quite sure how much Maggie knew—about the ash, about the tainted air and the coal company—or how much we ought to tell her.

I personally was thinking about me and Rose's parents on that morning, the morning the ash first fell. The looks on my mother and father's faces, dumbstruck—from sleepiness or from astonishment, I couldn't have been sure. They had only just awakened, had scarcely gotten dressed, and then maybe while still half-waking they had seen the gray stuff flitting against their windows, gathering like dust on their porch. Our porch. Our neighbors outside already, wandering lost in their own town, reaching with deadened arms up toward a metal-gray sky. Rose and I knew what the ash was because our parents had been talking about it for months by then, maybe years, about the power plant going up down the road from us. It'll poison the air, they said. It'll poison every one of us. But we wouldn't leave, because our parents had been born in Paradise and our parents' parents before them and their parents before them. Our whole family was buried in this town at the Adrie Hill Cemetery, and someday, we figured, we would be too, no matter how much money any company ever offered us.

It was a wonder the Gilmores hadn't left yet. Maggie had been sick as a baby, and now Mrs. Gilmore fretted over her constantly. If anyone was going to be bought out to leave Paradise for cleaner air in a foreign city, it was the Gilmores for sure.

"We'll come back here every day," said Joseph, ducking under a log that had fallen across the path. "Every day as long as we live, until we find Michael." He had been saying things along these lines since January, likely more for his own benefit than for anyone else's.

"It's summer now," Rose pointed out, "so that should make it easier." Her voice was toneless, as though she could barely even hear what she was saying.

"It's not summer yet," I said automatically. "Not 'til school's out."

"It's practically out. It feels like summer. We've only got a little bit left," Rose said, which was true. Only a little bit of school left and then we were out, free from any obligations, free to spend our days at the Green River for as long as we wanted and to eat watermelons and catch crawdads and sleep over at each other's houses. Just one long golden stretch of summer to make up for our schoolwork, for Michael and for the Tennessee Valley Authority, for all the winter we'd been going through lately. Joseph and I had plans to explore the power plant together as soon as we got a chance, hopefully with

Michael, although we weren't about to tell the girls that.

"Anyway," Rose said, "what I meant is that it's warmer than it was."

This was true. Michael had disappeared right after New Year's, when a lot of the river was still frozen over. The search parties from town, made up of all our fathers and mothers, had given up near the end of January, beginning of February, which was when the four of us had taken over. Trudging through snow and treading carefully on the icy stretches in February, then crunching over melting slush in early March. Thick boots and mittens and scarves to hide our necks. Breath materializing in front of us, taunting Michael's ghost, almost. *We're breathing, Michael. Are you?*

It took us until almost lunchtime to reach the part of the river we didn't know as well. Where the tangles of weeds and underbrush took on unknown shapes, where we came upon foreign forbidden flowers and plants, where the trees were alien and their dark branches bent oddly, all strange and sinister. At least it seemed that way to us. It had taken us a while to work up to this part of the river, since we were so in depth about everything—we could spend a whole day or two just at one spot, venturing further and further away from the water and into the trees, the four of us spreading out in each of the cardinal directions, bushwhacking sometimes as far as a mile.

We couldn't keep walking any later than one or two in the afternoon, or else we wouldn't be out of the woods until after dark. Joseph was the one with the watch. He stopped us at what he figured was a good spot, we all more or less agreed, and we dumped our backpacks in a pile in the grassy clearing next to the rushing water.

It was a rule among us that we ate lunch before we started looking, to refuel after the walk. We found places to rest—fallen logs and the knotted bases of trees, dry patches of grass—and sat in a loose circle facing one another, digging apples and aluminum-foil-wrapped sandwiches out of our backpacks.

"I hope we find him before summer," said Joseph as he unwrapped his sandwich, peanut butter smeared in the creases of the crumpled aluminum. "Or at least before July. It wouldn't be any fun to keep coming out here when it gets really hot out."

"Plus it wouldn't be any fun to have summer without him," said Maggie.

"That too," Joseph agreed. His mouth was full from chewing. He swallowed after a moment and then his mouth broke into a peanut-buttery grin. "Watch us find him—" He stopped, licked the brown stuff away from his teeth. "Watch us be out looking for him one day, and he just jumps up out of the water with a crawdad in his hand. Just splashes up out of the water, like, 'Hey look, guys, look how long I stayed under!'"

We had all memorized this mental image, partly I guess from having seen it in person so many times, but mostly from all the time we had spent over the last few months picturing it. Michael, drenched, clutching the clawing creature in his hand. Usually we'd all smile whenever somebody mentioned it, but today no one really responded.

"No one could hold their breath that long," said Rose.

"If anyone could," said Maggie with obvious reverence, "it'd be Michael." Maggie was in love with Michael, had been for years, got all doe-eyed whenever he was around. Every time she got sick, he'd drop by the Gilmores' and kiss her on the cheek, leave her apples and flowers, cards.

"*If anyone could, it'd be Michael,*" Joseph mocked her, tilting his head back, clasping his hands together and rolling his eyes as if in a dream.

Maggie shoved him. "Don't be mean."

"You shouldn't be so obvious," Joseph told her. "He's never gonna like you like that if he knows you like *him* like that."

"That's not how it works," said Maggie.

"Is too."

"You're right, Maggie, it's not," said Rose, talking to Maggie but looking at Joseph. "That's just how boys think it works."

"Oh yeah?" said Joseph. There was a little peanut butter just under his lower lip. He looked like he was trying not to smile.

"Yeah. Boys think they've gotta be mean to you or not talk to you, and that's how to get your attention. But all it's really doing is making them look like a bunch of babies."

"Not all boys are like that," I said.

"Not Michael," added Maggie.

"No," Rose agreed, "not Michael. He—he's better," she said, and then she looked quickly down into her lap as if to avoid making eye contact with any of us. She had been about to say *was*, I could tell—had been about to say, *He was better*.

We watched Joseph, waiting. He reached up and wiped the streak of peanut butter from his chin. "Yeah," he said then, finally. "Yeah."

We sat without talking for a few minutes. I could hear everybody chewing their food, and the river moving past and the trees shifting occasionally in the breeze. The air smelled rotten—not as bad as it smelled in town, but close—and I thought about the crawdads and wondered whether the water here tasted bad to them.

After a minute or so, I made eye contact with Rose. She had been staring into space looking blank, dejected, and only just then did I realize how much she, barely the oldest of all of us, resembled our parents. It wasn't even in how tall she'd gotten or anything like that—it was in the look on her face, so very much like the looks I'd seen on my mother's face and my father's that morning, as they stood in the ash falling under the white sky. Rose looked away as soon as she saw me watching her.

"Should we keep looking?" she asked. She crumpled her sandwich foil in her fist and slipped it inside her backpack, pulled the zipper shut.

And for some reason I felt really awful, for just a second then, like I wanted to cry. I stood, hoping to distract myself with a little movement, and kicked around at the grass while the others gathered themselves up. It felt like there was a yawn or something in the back of my throat, but by the time everyone was ready to keep searching it was gone.

I didn't know where it came from or what I'd been thinking until a few hours later. The day of searching ended with nothing, as it always did, and the woods had darkened by the time we straggled out again and scooped up our bikes. The sky was soft gray and humid, with none of the usual colors of sunset other than a faint yellow tinge over the tree line, and it felt like it might rain. Just ahead, I saw Rose do a gentle backpedal to brake and let Maggie catch up, her head ducked pensively and long brown hair fluttering back—and all at once, I knew that to Rose, Joseph and I were just like Maggie, young and hopeful, kidding ourselves. Rose already knew what our parents knew about Michael, about the power plant.

At that moment I thought I knew it too, and it made me angry. Let's just leave, then, I wanted to say. If all of this is such a lost cause, then let's give up. We all saw the ash. If we're not going to see the search through, if we're not going to see our own land through, our own town, then let's not stick around at all, not another single day.

I had seen those stricken looks on my parents' and on all our parents' faces only once before, the night Michael Harris disappeared back in January. We had just gotten through celebrating the new year, and Michael had gone back alone to the Green River to look for his gloves, which he'd forgotten there earlier in the day. By the dead of night he still hadn't returned, and one by one flashlights had flickered on like lanterns across town as we headed out of our houses to convene in the streets of Paradise. We walked to the river together as a crowd, a community, our beams of light arcing into still clusters of trees and casting blindly at patches of grass off the side of the road. *Michael! Michael, are you out there?* My family and the Gilmores, Mr. and Mrs. Harris, the Taylors, the Austins. The Buchanans, who were still standing their ground at that point and wouldn't be bought out until April. It was cold out and nobody felt like crying yet, we were just moving, out of the town and toward the river like ghosts, eyes wide open, insides numb, frozen.

    Some of us must have known that very night that the boy would never be recovered, that he'd be left behind with Paradise and the Green River forever just like the Adrie Hill Cemetery, while the rest of our houses and buildings were all torn down that year or the next to make room for the plant. The air we breathed was no good; it could not be sustained any longer. The McNamaras already knew this, and the Moores. Within a year, the Gilmores too would move east to Virginia,

Rose's and my family over to North Carolina. Most of us would never visit here again, knowing all too well what we would find—our landmarks buried under fat metal pipes and fenced facilities, the foul stench of machinery. By the time the ash fell, a strange feeling combined with the actions of the Tennessee Valley Authority had already splintered us, but on that January night Michael went missing we all moved together as a group, many of us even holding hands, the whole town staggered, venturing together toward the river and the pitch-black forest for as far as we could make it until dawn.

Pure Fear, American Legend

The girl is hitting a tennis ball against the brick outer wall of the gas station at the edge of town. Her shoulders hang loose; she hits the ball with force, like it might not hit her back. Quick repetitive slams. It seems like the sort of thing someone might stop her from doing, but no one is stopping her. A forehand, a backhand with a follow-through that arcs all the way up over her shoulder. The ball keeps racing back, and she keeps meeting it— focused, but with her eyes not quite on the ball itself, like she's in a trance. Her heels never touch the ground. In black Adidas shorts and a loose evergreen tank top, she bounces on the toes of her sneakers, long dark ponytail part-flipped over one shoulder and constantly relocating itself, flying with runaway frizz. She hops from side to side, eyes locking and relocking with brick, wielding the racquet again, again, shoes scratching over the cracked asphalt, oblivious to the mosquitos and the ads droning from the gas pump screens in the soft summery night and the people watching her.

There's a man standing over where the trucks are parked in their towering rows, leaning back against the body of a Werner semi and smoking; there's a man in too-thick glasses, idling in a green Volvo by the iceboxes with a dent in its fender; and there's Willa.

Her phone's dead, and she has nothing else to do. Willa rolls a mint around in her mouth, both hands in the pockets of her loose green jacket, and watches the solo rally from the opposite side of the lot while the tank of her Volkswagen fills. Between all the pillars and pumps and overflowing trash cans and strewn ashtrays, she catches only glimpses. A flash of ponytail, a determined glare, a swing.

She'd probably know the girl if she could see her face fully. Likely not a friend, though. Willa doesn't know anyone on the tennis team too well. She's never gravitated toward school sports—the competitiveness always felt like something better left to other people. She has no particular group at school, and she likes it that way. She has her collection of graphic novels no one else has quite read, her handful of friends no one else is quite friends with, and, recently, her boyfriend no one else is quite into. More than enough for this town, more than enough for the next two years. Clubs and sports are ways of getting locked into things—friend groups, uniforms, school spirit—and Willa likes being slippery, un-lock-downable.

But this girl is away from her uniformed friends, practicing alone and at the Chevron, of all places. Willa crunches the mint into dust, cranes her neck to see if she can get a look at who it is.

Suddenly the outside bathroom door opens, and a woman comes out in jeans and sunglasses and the tennis ball almost hits her in the face.

"Oh my god, I'm sorry," says the woman, stiffening.

"Oh my god," says the tennis girl, catching the ball on its rebound. "I'm so sorry!"

Willa knows that voice. The girl shifts into view then—and she knows that face, too. Sunny freckles, wavy hair, eyes that always look caught in headlights when Willa sees her get called on in math class. It's Phoebe Aimes. Willa doesn't really know her unless you count following her Instagram, which is mostly tennis practices, pastel-tinged mirror selfies and late-night flash Polaroids of Phoebe and Liz, her best friend.

The woman takes in the sight of the racquet, blinks, and shakes her head. "You're fine," she mutters. She hurries around to the Volvo by the iceboxes, where the man in the thick glasses is waiting in the driver's seat. She hops in, lets him drive her away.

Phoebe's hair is straying from its ponytail. She bounces the ball on her racquet, head dipping low again, and paces back over to a Subaru parked in the furthest row away.

Willa tries to shake herself loose from staring. She's not trying to be creepy. She just feels a little stuck.

The man over by the truck rows is also stuck, standing bowlegged in the shadows.

He looks thirty-five or forty. He'd be attractive, in a CW guy-at-the-bar sort of way, if not for the beard. He's wearing a thick corduroy jacket stained with coffee near the lap, and an oversized tee shirt underneath, with the name of a haunted house in Detroit printed over a corny flaming skull logo. PURE FEAR, reads the motto in ghostly white-green. AMERICAN LEGEND.

Yuck! Willa thinks as she watches him. And it's not the haunted house shirt or the stains or the beard—it's the way he's looking at the tennis girl, at Phoebe Aimes, while he slowly pulls the cigarette out of his mouth, lets the smoke fall into the air. Under the blazing light of the Chevron sign, the smoke flares before his face like a hazy halo. Through the cloud, his eyes don't move from Phoebe—she's tapping at her phone now, tracing thin lines in the dusty road with the toe of her purple tennis shoe, she's *clunk*ing the gas nozzle back in the pump, she's opening the backdoor of the Subaru and tossing her racquet in and shutting it. She's walking away from the car without locking it and to the gas station's front door, wallet twirling on her index finger.

Willa pulls her attention back again. Her car is full up. She replaces the nozzle and pops back in behind the wheel. She's running late. Brian will have picked out the movie already.

Over by the motionless trucks, the man drops his cigarette and puts it out with his boot.

Maybe Willa should start playing tennis. She could get fit, practice at gas stations. Of course, she'd need someone to practice with, but probably she could get Brian to do it. For a moment, she entertains the idea of trying it out, really getting good—and then one day running into Phoebe at another gas station or something, both of them practicing in tandem against a brick wall outside a disgusting bathroom. A game, or a match or whatever, ensuing between them, sprinting back and forth, competing on whatever court made itself available: an empty lot, a brick wall, an unused road. She smiles, starts the engine.

Only now, she sees that across the rows of pumps stretched between her and the Subaru, the man has crossed from the truck shadows into the fuzzed light of the gas station. He approaches Phoebe's SUV and glances in, and then, with one furtive, fruitless look around him, he climbs in and disappears into its backseat, the door closing quietly shut behind him. It almost didn't even happen.

Willa's brow furrows. Because—what? And already Phoebe is skipping out of the station with two Snickers bars clutched in one hand, her wallet and keys in the other. Willa opens her mouth; something is slamming against her forehead, knocking to get out. She can't convert it to words. In lieu of words she slams on her gas pedal and starts rounding the corner pump, almost scraping one of the pillars as a few rows off Phoebe hops into her SUV and pulls the door shut. Willa rolls down her window, already shouting something, but the Subaru is already pulling away from the pump, toward the main road. How can something like this feel so slow motion and then all at once so fast? How is she already gone?

"Hey! *Hey!*"

She's not gone. But she is lifting her cell phone up to her ear while she pulls onto the road, and between that phone call and the engines and wheels and the jangly ad music echoing off the pavement from the pump screens, when Willa finally finds another word and yells, "*Stop, come back!*" through her open window, she can't even see if Phoebe turns around.

***

When the call from Liz comes through, Phoebe's heart kicks around for a second in her chest, and she picks up right away.

"Hi, babe," says Liz while Phoebe accelerates, pressing past a yellow stoplight.

"Hey, you."

She's smiling already, which feels kind of stupid—but also fine, because she knows Liz would never think she was stupid. Liz would smile back.

"I don't know if I can come tomorrow night," says Liz.

"Oh. Oh?"

"Yeah." Liz's voice through the phone sounds scratchy, fabricated. "I really wanted to, but I was talking to Sean, and it turns out he's kind of got this whole thing planned—"

Phoebe lets her breath fall out slowly and silently and tries to listen. They were planning to have a bonfire in Phoebe's dad's yard tomorrow, just the two of them, with s'mores and Phoebe's guitar out under the stars. It's the perfect house for a bonfire, way out in the hills past the edge of town, with a half-mile-long gravel driveway bounded by rolling fields of tall grass and knotweed. Out there, the world of school feels less real. It's a place where rigid lines can fade and blur, where the stars peek out in numbers confidential to those rural areas and the people in them. Where secrets, maybe, can become known.

"Are you sure?" Phoebe asks. "There was something I kind of wanted to talk to you about—" She's not even sure why she says this part, when the decision's really already made, and immediately she feels like the clumsiest person ever.

Liz pauses, like she's thinking about it.

"Agh—yeah, Phoebs. I'm sorry. He wants to take me to the drive-in, and it might rain on Saturday, so tomorrow's the only night we can go. I'm so sorry. What if we did the bonfire next week, after tennis sometime?"

"On a school night?"

"Yeah!" Even Liz sounds only half-convinced, half-committed. "You've never had a sleepover on a school night? I think it could be fun."

Phoebe lets out a soft breath, glances at the thick, darkening trees lining the road as she rushes past them. The Indiana sky is steeped like tea, bleeding purple-red. The warmth of the night outside wants to hold something.

"Yeah," she says. "Sure."

"What'd you want to tell me? Could you tell me now?"

Phoebe considers it. Her muscles still feel sore and strong. She considers hurling the truth into the wall—*Fuck it*—and seeing what rebounds back to her. Whether she could handle it, if it went badly—if it hit her in the face and she tasted blood, or worse, if it sailed right over her shoulder and left her holding nothing forever.

Her heart claws back, like stilting herself from jumping off a quarry cliff at the last second. "It's not a big deal. I gotta go now, I'm driving," she says quickly. "But talk to you later?"

"Yeah." Liz exhales in what sounds like relief. "Thanks, Phoebs. I'm really glad you're not mad. I really wanted to come. I just couldn't."

Phoebe twists at the nickname. She hangs up but doesn't toss her phone to the passenger seat. She keeps holding it as she drives, clenching the plastic case.

A truck speeding the other way nearly drifts into her lane, and she jerks her steering wheel to the right and honks. Her tennis bag thumps in the backseat.

The truck swerves back into its own lane, and Phoebe exhales and flips on her headlights. Close call, she thinks as the car trailing her, a Volkswagen, moves closer.

***

Willa's cell phone is still dead, and she has no charger. Of course, she's that type of loser today. *Don't come any closer, man. My boyfriend's expecting me and he's going to notice I'm late any minute now and he's going to come here and find you and beat you up.* She's always thought of *beat you up* as something that was relatively easy, to the person with the most power, and happened quickly. But now she wonders how long it would really go on for. What would make it stop?

Anyway, Brian isn't really the beating-up type of boyfriend. He's barely the noticing type of boyfriend, or the general boyfriend type of boyfriend. He's Willa's first one, and she wasn't coming into the relationship with any sort of metric except that she ought to have one.

When Brian asked her to the Valentine's dance two months ago, it was the first time anyone had shown any real interest in her, and it awoke in her this excited, confused flutter—a mix between *this life is for me, this door has been opened* and *is that all?* She'd never wanted to date anyone—not really, not *wanted*. She didn't even really want to be wanted: that wasn't it, either. When she thought of things she actually wanted, she thought of a nice cold Sprite, or the little satisfaction of a solved calculus problem, or maybe, sure, a late summer day at Oberlin, or maybe even just some peace and quiet. A calm night to draw by herself, her family playing board games in the other room, occasionally asking her to join and not having their feelings hurt when she said no. She had those things already. She was a millionaire. She didn't yearn.

But she did want not to have the impression anymore that something was wrong with her. The sense that she was missing something crucial was starting to itch. Not often, but sometimes, she'd think things like *Damn isn't it funny how no one's ever really wanted me—not really, and all people ever do is want, just not me*—which wasn't even really true, but when something itches, you scratch it. She didn't want to be with someone just because they wanted her. That wasn't enough. It was a vacuum, wasn't it? It left both people still just doing all that wanting on both sides, and a steep drop-off between them, like always, but maybe they put a carpet over it.

So she decided to experiment. She went to Valentine's.

Too nervous, Brian didn't try to kiss her until their fourth date, an action movie matinee. Now they watch movies together on his couch and slip notes in each other's lockers, borrow sweaters, and she goes to all his cross-country meets. It's not extraordinary; she's still waiting on that *falling-in-love* feeling. It's true she loves Brian's sweetness and shyness, and his sense of humor which surprises her in group conversations when she's least expecting it. But sometimes she worries that she likes him most of all for how little trouble he causes her. How if she doesn't feel like calling or texting him, she doesn't have to. How easy it is to tell him sorry, or no.

So it really is Willa who's the villain, if she and Brian made plans for tonight and she's the one standing him up now, and she's the one who's flaked out on him so many times before, set the precedent, chosen her friends or family or just herself and neglected to tell him. He'll call once or twice and give up, and he absolutely won't question, tonight, whether she's in any danger. If she gets killed, he'll feel terrible. Very often this is just the way these things go.

She's afraid of wherever this will end, wherever they will both—all—get out of their cars. She knows the skeletons of stories like this: long country roads, full moons, dark nights. The same backdrops as love stories, really. Who will be the final girl tonight, if it comes right down to it? She has never thought of herself as someone who'd survive very long in a horrible situation. Is it really worth it for her to carry along down this road in the gathering nighttime, *she* being okay for the time being, *she* being fine, driving knuckles-first into the fifty-fifty risk of not being the girl who gets to go home to her boyfriend at the end of the night?

Now that she's here, so many coward's impulses stir inside Willa that she never even knew she had in her. (*Coward*, a part of her thinks, *or Any Reasonable Person?*) She's past the safe realm of gas stations and open businesses, but still, she could stop off the next time she sees someone's house off the road, yell at them to call somebody. But then what if the other car got away and was never found? Every time a house crops up with a short driveway or porch lights on, she tries to urge herself to stop—but then, each time, the driveway flicks past. She can't let go of the small thing she's holding. Can't shake the feeling she's already too late.

Her most fearful and shameful thought of all is what if she imagined the whole thing—it was a trick of the light, or maybe those two knew each other already, were traveling together, and this whole thing has just been Willa jumping to conclusions. A misunderstanding.

But the *backseat*. But the look on his face.

No, Willa isn't that tuned out, as much as she wishes it. She will have to honk at the Subaru or something, break the spell. If she beeps long and loud, Phoebe will pull over to let her pass, and then Willa will pull over, too—and then, what? A panic? A violence? Her fault? The moon, which she had thought she could trust, might hit her over the head.

She thinks she sees a flash of motion in the back row of the Subaru, and she flicks on her headlights, her heart tumbling over itself and down the stairs. The softest warning.

***

Phoebe makes the first turn off the main road. The roads out here are smaller and emptier, more winding, but she doesn't slow down. She knows every curve, knows where to look out for deer.

The Volkswagen follows her down, headlights carving around the corner.

It's been there for what feels like a while, but Phoebe shrugs it off. Because Liz: how is it that Liz—someone she loves so much—is like this?

Phoebe can't blame her, or knows she *shouldn't* blame her, for having crushes and pursuing them and in particular flaking out on seeing the new Marvel movie so she could play video games with Sean and his brothers. Or asking Phoebe to cover for her so she could walk around downtown with Sean all night and watch the sun rise from the top of the parking garage, Leon Bridges playing through the narrow speaker of Liz's iPhone until it died—not checking in with anyone, pretending their whole lives could be like this. That's what teenagers *do*. It's just not what Phoebe does.

Phoebe's pretty, and can feel herself becoming only prettier by the day. She has never felt pretty before this year, but looking at her now, the way she carries herself, one would think she simply grew up this way. It could be that it's all in the way she looks at herself, because when she looks back at old photos, she *can* easily trace the similarities in her features between then and now—but to her it seems almost indisputable that now, her junior year of high school, she has finally cracked all the gateways to beauty that were previously withheld from her. One by one, she's taught herself the practices and rituals of using lotion to keep her skin smooth; washing her hair with the right shampoo, the right conditioner, according to the right frequency, knowing when to brush it and when to just run her fingers through; trimming and plucking her eyebrows and filling them in with the right pencil; smoothing and filling out her features with foundation, highlighter, blush and finishing powder. Her mother lives in Ohio, and she has no older sisters. Everything Phoebe has, she figures, right or wrong, she's given to herself. Once, years ago, she looked in a gym locker room mirror at herself next to a bunch of other scrawny middle-school girls and witnessed her scabby knees, her stringy hair, her baggy shorts and tee shirt next to their crisp Adidas ensembles, and she hated what she saw, truly hated it. And who changed all that but her? One piece of herself at a time? Who made her someone worth loving? She tried painstakingly, the more she thinks about it, over years, just to *fit*, and now she *does*—only this year has she felt like she really fits. But the only thing she really wants to fit, it feels like now, is Liz, and she isn't there.

When people flirt with Phoebe now, she feels a mix of pleasure and resentment. Of course, she thinks, people are attracted to her. Who wouldn't be—truly, who? She knows she's vain and getting vainer, but she thinks of it as an earned vanity. One she has worked for and would like to let herself savor.

But the other spark that goes off in her head, when boys grin at her through the tennis court fences or nudge up against her pretend-accidentally at dances or approach her in the tile hallways, is *I see right through you.* If her choice is to join all this, she would almost rather never be seen again by anyone.

The Volkswagen is still right behind her. Brights flick on, a blinding flash in her rearview mirrors.

"Okay," she mutters, under her breath in the quiet car. "Chill already."

The SUV rocks as the road turns to gravel, and she thinks she hears another bump—a pothole.

Her phone lights up in the passenger seat: Liz's grinning face in front of their favorite ice cream shop, holding a cone of the only flavor she ever orders, mint chip with chocolate sprinkles, her blonde curls bunchy and thick around her head. Phoebe lets it ring a few times. There is usually something about a call from Liz, or a text from Liz, that she simply cannot ignore, but this time she does.

The brights behind her flick and flick, ten minutes, now, from home.

***

Willa's knuckles on the steering wheel have gone bald, paper-white. She's sure she saw something a moment ago: a bump of a shadow, rising in the backseat of the car.

She will never sleep again after this, she promises herself. She will shine her phone light in every closet of whatever house she sleeps in, lock her car four times before she walks away from it.

She knows the story she's in, that's the ridiculous part. She had the *Hang on a sec* moment, the *I've heard this one before*. A guy gets into a girl's car with a knife in hand, and another guy follows her home, flashing his headlights every time the intruder sits up to kill the girl. A little weird, when Willa thinks about it—who, even if they're a murderer, wants the driver of the car they're inside to suddenly get stabbed? It sounds dangerous, she thinks squarely.

Anyway, at the end of the story everyone gets out, and the police come, and there's a punchline—*it's not ME you should be arresting*, says the guy following her, pointing to the backseat, *it's HIM*—but that's all Willa can remember. Presumably the girl is fine, right? But do they fight him off? How do they win?

Not that knowing would do her any good, now. She rests a hand on the center of the wheel, almost presses the horn, then almost presses again, then almost presses again. Does she have any weapons in the car? She wonders this again, as if checking again will change the answer. Anything she might use? No—not really; just herself. These hands. Hmm.

Sharp tears glaze her eyes, but she refuses to blink and make them real, which makes the sting worse. Every few seconds, through the pitch-black trees, she catches a sliver of the moon. Stop all this, stop, stop, she thinks, an anesthetic, but of course, because she's here to help, she presses down on the gas instead.

***

Phoebe turns on the radio, and it's a love song, or that's what she hears it as—but Phoebe knows in the right mood, she can hear the weirdest things as love songs. Right now it's "American Girl" by Tom Petty. There's only one good station here and it's classic rock, the same forty or fifty tracks always on a rotation.

Phoebe has no right to feel optimistic, but she does when this song comes on. It floods her with the type of sadness that is so forceful, it pushes angrily into joy—one of those vivid, electric feelings only good music brings, which will pass by tomorrow but feels like the only real thing on the planet now. It's a raging happiness that rots at its core. It's the feeling of, *there's no beauty here, in what I'm feeling—what I'm feeling is gross and there's nothing good in it at all.* The bonfire is off, and Sean Blake is somehow miles more beautiful than her even though he doesn't do anything, he doesn't do *anything*, and she loves Liz. Really, she does. She thinks of the meet where Liz fell asleep on the nighttime bus ride into Phoebe's shoulder and how much it ached, how it peeled her heart away. The look in her eyes when she listens. She thinks of Sean Blake and what the look in Liz's eyes must be when she listens to him, too, just the two of them, perfect evenings to perfect music, and then Phoebe rams up the volume and rolls down the window and thinks, FUCK *it*, screams over the drums, "FUCK *it*," things are going to be all right—they really are. She's going to be all right. She can get better anywhere, even if it's just in some ugly corner where no one's watching. And she will.

Like she often does when she hears this song, she remembers the scene from *The Silence of the Lambs*—she watched it with Liz, actually, who likes horror and has been trying to get her into it. Phoebe can't stand it. It's all way too creepy. She is already paralyzed with fear over the most basic parts of her life, and she sees no good reason to add to it. But she's seen *The Silence of the Lambs* and she knows the scene where the girl's in the car screaming along to "American Girl"—the one time, really, that that girl is happy in the whole movie—and then just afterward, she gets coaxed into that guy's van and knocked out and kidnapped. Phoebe hated that scene. But she thinks of it now and screams the lyrics—the fact that she's seen that movie and is still here now, on a dark road alone at night, singing that same song at the top of her lungs, this is how she knows she is brave. Surely brave enough to talk to her best friend, if she can sing this song, this loud, on a night this creeping and dark.

    The other car is right up on her tail now, can probably hear the music and her joy. Good, she thinks, let someone take it. Through the music she hears honking, long and loud and insistent. The other car's beeps come staccato, almost frantic, but in the wash of song and nighttime-drive-exclusive anger, she figures, what-the-fuck-ever. She keeps driving.

It's the deer that stops her, like a cutout in the sudden catch of her headlights, standing stolid in the middle of the dirt-gravel road. Facing her straight-on. It doesn't move from the narrow path even when the light swoops over it. Phoebe slams her brakes and tries veering to the side, hoping the car behind her will stop too or else veer with her. When the thump comes, there's a moment when she doesn't even know who has collided with whom.

***

The first time Willa went out with Brian, at the Valentine's dance, she wore sparkling gray eyeshadow and grapefruit lip gloss and a sequined sapphire-blue dress her mom helped her pick out from the clearance rack at Macy's, a size too small around her waist. She picked Brian up with his mousy hair brushed and his navy shirt tucked in, his terrified smile. Willa got so nervous beforehand, just like on her first day of high school, when she kept shaking in the steam of her hair straightener mixed with the cold of the air conditioning and she thought she might throw up in the bathroom. But at the dance, there were frosted sugar cookies, blue square napkins, and all Willa's friends. She could tell Brian was twice as scared as she was, which was sweet. Don't think about how nervous *you* feel, she remembers thinking to herself at one moment, in a beautiful revelation. Think about how to make him feel better. It was a means to an end, and it helped her step magically into another heart. It's okay, she thought, you can just be this now. She hasn't seen herself since.

***

Out stumbles Willa in a rush, fists-forward—she feels like a moron, but doesn't know what else to do. She figures she will die fists-first. Phoebe is confused, still in her car. "He's gonna kill you," Willa blathers, "get out, he's gonna kill you—" She yanks aside the SUV back door and the man's already there, scrambling up and out—she might see some panic in his eyes, too, after all, maybe he's never done this before—maybe they're *all* new to this—but the time and the world in which she would've cared to know his side of the story have both passed, he's forfeited them. He could've lived a whole life and this violence would still make no sense to Willa. He launches his body onto Willa's and pins her back, and pain curls up her spine at the impact. He smells sweaty, feels heavy, looks kind of normal up close only because she can see his blue eyes, except that it's so dark out and this isn't normal. He's trying to knock her out, maybe, grappling for the upper hand, trying to keep her arms pinned down while the sharp edges of scattered gravel dig into her back. He tries getting a hold of her hair, slamming her head back into the dirt ground, but it's not hard enough, does nothing. Willa tries yanking her knee up into his groin, but that doesn't work either, she can barely even move under the weight of him. They both feel so awkward. She flails and kicks and rolls, feeling helpless and idiotic, like in P.E. last year when she had to try to figure out fucking football alongside all those assholes—and then she starts crying while she thrashes her arms up between her face and this stranger's, both of them trying to get a grip on each other, because what if she never gets to try playing fucking football again, and what if— what if Brian is up right now, on his couch, in his lit, warm living room—what if he feels sad—because she's not with him—like she said she would be, and maybe because of that he thinks she doesn't love him like she does.

The tire iron comes down out of nowhere, hitting the man where his neck arcs into his spine. Neither of them sees it coming. Dull shock shoots through the blue eyes, and his panicky-tight grip on her arms slackens. She jostles and squirms out, back, away from under him, like he's an enormous insect that's landed on top of her body.

The trunk of the Subaru is open, the light on inside. In front of it, Phoebe Aimes is crouching and crying. Her hands out between her and Willa, one of them still loosely gripping the iron, but not touching Willa, as if afraid to, asking, *Oh my god, are you okay? Are you okay?*

Willa scoots back over the gravel and then up, sort of, to her feet. Imbalanced, she grabs one of Phoebe's hands and lets her help her. The man is still on the ground, knocked out. There's a deep gash just under his left eye socket; it strikes Willa that the scratch, at some point, was from her own fingernails.

"I'm so sorry," Phoebe is saying, over and over. "I'm so sorry."

Willa snaps her fingers in front of her own face, to bring herself back. "What?" she says to her hands. "Why?"

"I don't know. I—"

"You're fine. Agh," says Willa, at nothing in particular. She turns around where she's standing, considers vomiting but can't quite muster anything. "Jesus."

"It was my tire iron," says Phoebe, the words pouring out of her. "For—emergencies."

"You have your phone?"

"Oh." Phoebe hesitates, as though afraid to move away from Willa and the unconscious man. Then she hurries over to the passenger seat of her car, pulls out an iPhone and dials while walking back over, her pace wobbly.

Willa is still staring down at the man, breathing hard. She can feel the dirt all over her—mussed in her hair, stamped into the back of her jeans and her tee shirt. The little red dents of skin where the gravel pricked her, already fading, and a more twisting pain in her right arm and up her shoulder. Where she was pushing against him, away.

Phoebe starts speaking into her phone—her voice becoming shakier, now, with each sentence—and while she waits, Willa paces across the gravel. She finds the deer lying in front of the Subaru's fender. She crosses over to get a look at its matted fur, illuminated in the car's headlights. The deer is breathing shallowly, belly lifting up and drifting down, wet black eyes casting around in the night.

"Poor sweet thing," Willa mutters as Phoebe hangs up the phone. It must, she thinks, be very bright. She straightens and hurries around Phoebe's driver's side, finds the headlights knob and flips them off. Then she comes back around, squats next to the deer in the darkness, like a detective huddling by a crime scene. Phoebe walks over to her.

They sit in the gravel road between the deer and the man, the two limp bodies of the night. "I wish I hadn't hurt it," says Phoebe mournfully.

Willa tries to think of something she could say to slip away from how heavy she feels. "Reckless driving," she says. "Something was bound to happen."

Tears start spilling from Phoebe's eyes, looking at the deer.

"Oh, my God. I wasn't serious, this wasn't your fault." Willa extends her arms, leaving the hug up to Phoebe, who leans in.

Phoebe whispers into her shirt, "My dad's going to be so mad."

"Oh my God, stop. Are you kidding? He's gonna be proud as hell. You did the perfect thing."

Neither one of them says, *You saved my life*. "Come on," says Willa then, standing up and lifting Phoebe along with her by her arm. They walk slowly back around to Willa's car, in full view of any oncoming traffic. The road isn't one way, but it's narrow enough to feel like it, the shadowed muscles of maples and larches and sycamores pressing close in on both sides. They rustle with the density of night, a few stars perched far off in the canopy. This summer's cicadas raise a raucous wall of sound around the road, their year finally here, mixing with the crickets that around May start forming the background of everything around here.

Very far off somewhere in all of it are the lights of distant houses, which Willa didn't see before, but now they peek like searchlights down the road.

"You live in the middle of nowhere."

"Yeah."

"I saw you playing tennis," says Willa. "Back at the gas station. I recognized you—you were good." She really doesn't know what it looks like to be good, especially when you're playing by yourself, and your opponent is a brick wall. But Phoebe looked dedicated.

"Thanks," says Phoebe. She doesn't look gratified or even really distressed anymore. She just looks, for now, a little confused. "You're Brian Lang's girlfriend, right? What's your name?"

"Willa." She feels a weird detachment from it, like she's naming not herself, not her life, but this thing that just happened.

Red and blue dots appear down the road, swirling like disco lights in a fast-gathering glow. Only against the sirens does Phoebe give a sudden, small jolt and walk back over to the Subaru, reach in through the open window and turn off the radio. Neither of them noticed it was still playing. The crickets take up the gap.

"Oh!" says Phoebe, still ducked inside the car, her voice muffled behind the windshield.

She reemerges holding two small identical objects—*sticks* is Willa's first thought. Phoebe tosses one over. It's a Snickers bar.

Willa laughs hoarsely. "Like I'm gonna eat."

"What do you mean?"

"I feel like I could throw up right now."

"You have to eat," says Phoebe mildly. She opens her wrapper with a dainty peeling motion, without quite looking at it. "I've got water in the car, too. You gotta take care of yourself."

Willa slips the candy bar in her pocket for later. Standing between the cars, she sees the few patches of blood in the dirt where before the deer was lying.

She doesn't see the deer now, not even in the grassy shadows where the trees meet the road, not even as a motion. She wonders where it went. She must have gone somewhere too, when it disappeared; she'd thought she was standing here the whole time, but then she should've seen it vanish. She must have been somewhere else. Phoebe walks up to stand beside her as the car speeds their way, sirens rising, the man still lying in the road.

Willa can no longer remember what story she was thinking of, or what song was playing on the radio. She tilts her head, rolling it around to dissolve some of the pain in her neck and the top of her spine. She tries counting the branches fanning over the road, then the headlights weaving their way through the trees. In her head they're so close they're almost the same, the brightness and friction drawing them together like water, but then she blinks and they click apart again. One two.

Willa squats very low for a moment, drums her fingers sharply along her hairline. She stands back up. "I can't do it," she whispers.

"Do what?" says Phoebe, but her tone isn't like she wants an answer, and as she says it, she slings one arm around Willa's shoulders. She squeezes her arm in a half-hug for a moment and lets go. The air between them shivers.

Thank You

It's hard to express how much I owe to the people around me. Thank you to my family for always being my biggest supporters in every way, and for reading my writing and listening to me talk about it throughout my life. To my parents and siblings, my grandparents, my aunts and uncle and cousins: I love being around all of you, no matter what I'm doing or where we are, and it's so easy to be creative and excited about the world when I'm with you.

Thank you to all the writing teachers I've had, throughout high school and at the University of Michigan and Indiana University. I was so lucky to have teachers who took my writing seriously when I was young and encouraged me to do the same. You all continue to impact my life in enormous ways. Gina, you are one of the best teachers I've ever had. Thank you to Samrat, Brando, Michelle, Ross, and Romayne for your help on early versions of many of these stories, and for the atmospheres you created in workshops in grad school. Michelle, Alexander, and Michael, thank you for being willing to read this book and write words of support; I have learned so much from all your work. Thank you to my own students; you all have challenged me, woken me up to the possibilities of literature, and inspired me with your care for the written word and for each other.

Thank you to all the friends who've read books with me, and to my fellow writers and workshop peers of all genres. Thank you to Kali and everyone from my Tin House workshop who made the conference so fruitful and helpful and warm, even on Zoom! Thank you to Matt and the other editors who've put time, thought, and heart into their work with me, even just on a single piece. Thank you to all my colleagues and new friends and writing mentors from this new time in Massachusetts—I can't believe how much I've already learned from you in such a short time. You remind me how linked writing and loving are. The care you put into your teaching and your work with literature raises my standards for myself and moves me daily.

Thank you to my friends for making me the person I am. Janice, Julia, and Clarissa, I don't even know what to say; I hope you all know how much you've changed my life. Laura #1, thank you for always making me smile and always being there. Julia, you are the most ferociously loving person I know. Ellie, you know this book would literally not exist without you. When I don't know who I am, you do. I wish I could give all of you everything you deserve and more, because you have given so much to me.

Susanna, your impact on my life has been immeasurable; I lived with you during one of my hardest times, and being around you made me keep loving things. I love your astounding level of daily commitment to art and to your loved ones. I couldn't have dreamed of a more fitting cover for this collection; I'm honored that you were willing for this book to be ours.

Thank you, Niall, for wanting to read this book! Your enthusiasm brings to the surface the things I most love about myself. Thank you for waiting patiently as I type this too! I love sharing happiness with you.

Thank you to the entire team at Sundress for your passion for this book. Some of this process happened to coincide with a time I've felt relatively distant from my own writing, but your enthusiasm for this project has given me so many crucial reminders. I am especially grateful for your insistence that I am happy with the final product, and for your extreme patience with my response time to emails.

I learned so much of how I relate to the world in Indiana. I have so much love for the woods—I almost wrote "here," and then remembered that I'm typing this in Colorado, but "here" feels right because Indiana is always with me. I love the fireflies and the soy and cornfields and the sassafras and maple and oak trees. I love the fire tower and the lake. I love spring, summer, fall, and winter, the sounds of mourning doves and the thick crickets that shelter me at night. I love the frogs who don't need me to see them; I love them by their sound. I love humidity and the way deer stand. I love the little ladybugs and grasshoppers and the spiders.

I love my childhood dogs, Elvis and Chino and Benny, who were all so good in such different ways, and Cody, the most intense cat ever, and my cat Eleanor, who I only needed to see to feel like everything was okay. And my cat now, Merry, who is so much fun to take care of; when I look back on times when I've felt stressed or anxious or unproductive, she reminds me I spent those times loving someone.

Thank you to anyone and everyone I haven't named here. This was one of the hardest parts of this book to write. I don't know how to fit the people I love into a Thank You page; you all are in this whole book. You're in everything I do. It is the honor of my life to be in the families I'm in, and to have the friends I have, and to be living on this Earth.

About the Author

Laura Dzubay is a writer and teacher from Indiana. Her stories and essays have appeared in *Electric Literature*, TIMBER, *Gulf Coast*, *Mid-American Review*, *Cimarron Review*, *Blue Earth Review*, and elsewhere. She earned her MFA from Indiana University, where she won the AWP Intro Prize. She loves music, camping, and hiking, and in 2022, she completed a thru-hike of the Appalachian Trail.

Other Sundress Titles

Ruin & Want
José Angel Araguz
$17.99

Little Houses
Athena Nassar
$16.00

In Stories We Thunder
V. Ruiz
$12.99

Slack Tongue City
Mackenzie Berry
$12.99

Sweetbitter
Stacey Balkun
$12.99

Cosmobiological: Stories
Jilly Dreadful
$16.99

I Am Here to Make Friends
Robert Long Foreman
$14.99

the Colored page
Matthew E. Henry
$12.99

Year of the Unicorn Kidz
jason b. crawford
$12.99

Something Dark to Shine In
Inès Pujos
$12.99

Slaughter the One Bird
Kimberly Ann Priest
$12.99

What Nothing
Anna Meister
$12.99

www.ingramcontent.com/pod-product-compliance
Lightning Source LLC
Chambersburg PA
CBHW051254230125
20710CB00010BA/144